MW01265619

VISIONS

Kimberly Readnour

Printed by CreateSpace

Printed by CreateSpace

Author's Note: This is a work of fiction. Names, characters, places, and incidents are a product of the author's imagination. Locales and public names are sometimes used for atmospheric purposes. Any resemblance to actual people, living or dead, or to businesses, companies, events, institutions, or locales is completely coincidental.

Book Layout ©2013 BookDesignTemplates.com
Edited by Kathie Middlemiss of Kat's Eye Editing
Cover Design by SelfPubBook.Com/Shadel

Visions/ Kimberly Readnour. 1st ed.
ISBN 978-1503072381

To my daughter. I love you more than the universe and beyond.

CONTENTS

Prologue

A faint sound—perhaps a whimper—echoes faintly in the background of my mind. Seconds, or maybe hours later, the sound returns, ringing annoyingly through my head. I'm desperate for it to go away. It takes a few more moments for me to realize the annoying sound is coming from my very own mouth. Something isn't quite right, but I'm too unfocused to figure out what.

I wonder where I am while mentally questioning what happened to me, but I'm groggy and confused. I feel dominated, trapped by the total darkness surrounding my mind. I can't move, rendered motionless from my semi-conscious state on the hard, unfamiliar surface. It's as if my brain can't process what I'm lying on, making me question my location, and how I even got here—wherever here is. Though I can't seem to remember anything, deep down I know I'm not here by choice.

An urgent need to know where I am is overpowering as my brain finally registers the necessity of opening my eyes. If I could see my surroundings, then perhaps I'll be able to recognize where I am. Taking a deep breath, I use what little strength I have to force them open. They barely budge. Defeat washes through me as I realize my eyelids are heavy, the simple task of opening them is impossible. *What's wrong with me? Why can't I move?*

Part of the problem is my head...my head is pounding, it hurts so bad. It feels as if someone's taking a drumstick and beating on top rhythmically. Boom...Boom...Boom...If I bring my hands to my forehead, I could apply enough pressure that may disperse the pain. I try raising them, but my arms won't cooperate. I can barely lift them off the ground. *Where did all my energy go?*

I'm not sure what to do next because this pain isn't leaving. I inhale a deep breath and hold it while reopening my eyes. A sharp pain darts straight across my head, landing right between them. It takes all my strength to not wince while closing them tight in hopes of helping, having little success.

Deflated, I lie perfectly still for a few more minutes, taking slow, even breaths. I begin to realize I have two options. Either continue to lay here without moving, or try to figure out what's happened to me. After a few seconds of debate, I opt to go with the latter.

With yet another deep breath, I force my eyelids open as far as I can manage, trying my hardest to ignore the agony, but everything's dark and blurry. Deep in my chest, a burning sensation emerges, as if any minute the suppressed panic that has been simmering is going to burst out. I squeeze my eyes shut again, for the pain has become unbearable. Another soft whimper escapes.

Maybe I should just continue to lie still. Focus on something other than torment. Breathing...I need better control of my breathing, for it has accelerated to the dangerous level of hyperventilating. I keep telling myself to calm down and get a grip. Focus on taking slow, deep breaths. The more I breathe in, I realize, the more I'm nauseated. Ugh...That smell. It stinks of stagnant, damp air, mixed with stale cigarette smoke. I force myself to pace my breaths anyway, cringing at the scent while the question of my location lingers in my mind.

My sense of hearing isn't helping me figure anything out as I slowly begin to realize this quietness isn't normal. It has an eerie presence about it. As I strain to recognize any noise that would hint at my location, I realize the only audible sounds are coming from me. I need to remember what my last steps were. In an instant my heart starts beating faster as pieces of last night flash through my mind. A guy. I remember a guy in a black coat, who appeared rather suddenly behind me.

It all comes flooding back, washing over me like a tidal wave, as I begin to remember...*I was leaving the mall last night, crossing the parking lot to get to my car. The sun had set, making the area seem more deserted and threatening than usual. The darkness made me regret my choice of parking in such a desolate area. Upon arriving, it didn't seem bad, but as I was leaving, uneasiness stirred inside from being the sole person around. I decided to call my best friend, Kelsey, to keep me company as I walked across the blackened pavement. By the time we finalized our plans for the next evening, I had approached my car. With each closer step, my confidence had grown to the point of feeling secure enough to end our conversation.*

While I stood there digging around my purse for my keys, I could hear Mom's criticizing voice in the back of my head saying, "April, you should always be prepared." Wanting to curse at her for constantly being right, I paused after hearing a shuffling sound coming quickly behind me.

Upon glancing up, I flinched as a reflection suddenly appeared in my car window. My heart rate spiked at the realization of being in trouble, for the image revealed a man wearing a long, black coat, standing directly behind me. Before I could do anything else, I found myself struggling with him as he quickly overpowered me. Although he was much stronger, I kept squirming to get out of his control. I defiantly opened my mouth to scream, but a cloth emerged from his hand, concealing my face. I tried not to breathe, knowing it would be too dangerous, but I couldn't hold my breath any longer. As soon as I inhaled, a strong chemical odor engulfed my senses. An intoxicating, heady scent enveloped me, making me unsteady as the ground started spinning under me. It didn't take too long before I became weaker and weaker as I succumbed to the total blackness that overcame my body...

A tingling sensation jolts through me, causing me to shiver at the recall of that last memory. This snaps me back into the present, here and now...wherever here is. I want to cry, but that isn't going to help me. I tell myself to be strong and find a way out of here. Try to escape. I keep repeating this to myself, like a *self-help* pep talk, but what I need to do first is move.

With my eyes fluttering, and body shaking, my brain registers that I'm cold. As I placed my hands against the floor, an understanding crosses my mind...I'm lying on a slab of cooled, damp concrete. *Why couldn't I figure that out before?* With my cheek flat against the ground, I seem to be getting colder with each passing minute, now that I'm aware of it.

I need to get up; it's the only way to get better, but lifting my head is impossible. It's so heavy. All I can manage is to raise it a few inches off the ground. I swear an anvil is sitting on top of my shoulders, where my head should be. Giving up, I lower it back down, and try reopening my eyes instead. The pain is persistent, refusing to go away, but I desperately try to ignore it. The only thing visual is blackness, but despite the pain they somehow manage to remain open.

As things slowly begin to come into focus, it's a miracle I can finally see. After scoping my surroundings, my nose crinkles in disgust, doubting there are any miracles performed here. The eerie darkness of the room sends another shiver through my body as I lay here thinking that this definitely isn't a place I would voluntarily come. This is a place I would run far away from.

My eyes close for a second to recollect my thoughts. Upon reopening them, they shift toward my left, noticing a faint light coming in from a small window. *Could it be morning already? God, how long have I been down here?* As I continue to stare at the window, a sensation of hope sweeps through me. Maybe, just maybe, it offers a way for escape. If I can figure out where I am, I might have a chance.

With all my strength, I endure the throbbing pain and somehow manage to sit. The dizziness hits as the room starts swirling, forcing me to stay still. This spinning is making me queasy, as if I could throw up. I make myself take slow, deep breaths in and out, in hope to ward off the nausea. Although the stale, foul air isn't helping too much, the slow breaths calm my stomach. At least the pounding in my head has started to diminish.

As my body becomes adjusted to being upright, I glance back toward the window. I need to get over there. Inhaling deeply, I begin to stand. My legs shake badly, making every move more difficult. I keep my focus on the window, ignoring the tingling sensations shooting up my legs. I have to see out of that window.

I somehow manage to wobble over toward the filtered light. The lack of strength in my legs, along with the lack of visibility, is making me move slowly, but at least I'm moving. The faint light shining in, and my not fully adjusted eyes, offer little help. I breathe a sigh of relief when I'm just about there. Only having a couple of more steps to go, I stumble over a crate hidden in the shadows. At first wanting to curse it, I quickly realize it could be used to my advantage. Slowly scooting it underneath the sill, I step on to it. What little hope I have quickly vanishes, as the scenery offers no chance of escape. Big iron rods cover the outside of the window, crushing all hope of crawling out.

Defeated, I peered further out the window, noticing a lake. *Is this Desti Lake?* I quickly scan the area for some type of distinguishing features, trying to find some type of verification of my whereabouts. Although I doubt I'll recognize much from here, since the only section of the lake I've been to is the beach.

The beach…a lump develops in my throat as I find myself trying to hold back my tears at the warm memories of my friends at the beach. The very thought of never seeing them again is almost too much for me to comprehend. Blinking my eyes to stop the tears forming, I continue to peer out the window. Just as I suspected, nothing is recognizable. I happen to see a log cabin house across the way. The house is one story, not elaborate, and a little run down. Down the path in front of it, more toward the edge of the lake, sits a fake lighthouse. Disappointment sets in as this information doesn't help me.

If I could see beyond the side of the house, then maybe something might come into view that would help. As I stretch out and lean toward my left, I wobble slightly, causing the crate to scoot out from underneath me. I land on the floor with a big thud, causing panic to rush through my body as I realized that I've just made a tremendous amount of noise. My head whipped upward toward the ceiling as fear overcomes me from the sound of running footsteps overhead.

Quickly scooting away from the window, I knew my chances of survival were slim. My head turns sharply toward the stairs as the squeak from the door pierces through the deafening silence. My breath caught as my pulse quickens from the appearance of a dark figure on the top of the stairs. The clicking sound of the light switch causes me to flinch as I struggle with my breath. Soft amber light creates shadows throughout the room from the single light bulb hanging from above. Although I wouldn't think it possible, it makes the place seem dirtier, even more sinister.

Home quickly flashes through my mind, along with images of Mom and Dad. It's a safe haven, a place where I'm secure and loved. Longing to be there, I know in the back of my mind it wasn't going to happen. I'll never know the safety of my loved ones again.

Unable to breathe, my heart continues to race, leaving me paralyzed. Trapped as I sit here, completely useless. Although knowing it's solely from fear, I can't move, regardless. Not sure how much more I can handle before my heart decides to explode like a ticking time bomb, I continue sitting as if frozen.

Move, April, I tried yelling at myself without success. You need to move.

As he draws closer, I know I need to do something or at least try to get away. Regardless, that doesn't seem to be helping me move. Fight or flight...words I've heard many times throughout my life, not ever giving them a second thought. Fight or flight...I know I need to do something quickly. Instead, I keep sitting here useless, completely immobilized.

As the guy's face comes into focus, my eyes grow wider from the shock of recognition. My school is where I know him. He's the custodian's assistant. Questions quickly begin swirling through my mind, like why would he do this to me? What is he going to do? Still breathless, I continue sitting here, paralyzed by the fear overpowering my body as he leans in closer toward me. His dark, blackened eyes penetrate through me as his arms stretch out to grab me. *Why can't I move?* Just as he's about to wrap his fingers around my arms, I find my voice, letting out a blood-curdling scream.

1   Fresh Beginnings

"Well, Heather, what do you think? Isn't it perfect?" Mom gushed.

I could tell she was nervous about my reaction because her words were rushed. The lack of direct eye contact was so obvious that I bit my lower lip to keep from rolling my eyes. Taking a deep breath, I reminded myself to be patient with her since she was trying to please me. The move, regardless of what I thought about it, had been entirely her idea. "A new start is just what you need," she repeated over the last few months. Finally putting her words into action, we packed up and moved four hundred miles away from the one place I'd ever known, to this quaint, historical town.

In some ways, the move had been all too simple. First, Mom was a nurse, making it easy for her to find a job anywhere. Second, with just being the two of us for most my life, we didn't have any other family to worry about. My father disappeared when I was six years old, leaving my mom to raise me on her own. Honestly, I didn't have a clue whether he was alive or dead, nor did I care. He hadn't tried to contact us since he left, which made me consider him dead. Mom never brought up the subject, and I never asked.

Both sets of Grandparents had passed long before I was born, leaving us with hardly any family. One aunt— my biological father's sister—was living, but we hadn't spoken to her in years either. After my father left, she called once in a while in a half-attempt to keep in touch. That didn't last long, as her calls became further and further apart, until they stopped altogether. I wasn't sure if Mom even knew her address anymore. It wasn't like we were concerned.

"This is great, Mom, exactly what we need," I said with a pathetic attempt to smile.

My words were enough to appease her because a huge grin broke across her face. One thing I'd learned this past year was to tell people what they wanted to hear. That was the easiest way.

Besides, she didn't want to know how I *really* felt. She wanted a sugar-coated version, that life would suddenly be perfect. Unfortunately, everything was far from perfect. In my opinion, moving was the same as running away from the challenges life had thrown at you. Since problems don't exist in the euphoric world she envisions, my life would never measure up because it would always be problematic. I wasn't sure if she thought my *predicament* would disappear by simply changing our location, but it didn't quite work that way. I'd still be different from everyone else, a *freak,* as I was often called.

I didn't mean to sound unreasonable. I understood what Mom was trying to accomplish. She wanted me to have a fresh start or "new beginning" as she called it. One where people wouldn't know about my special talent.

She just went about it wrong. My therapist told me to be patient and keep an open mind about the move, which was what I was trying to do, but as I inspected our new house, I found it rather difficult.

"Right through here is your room. It has a wonderful view of the woods, which is why I thought you'd like it." Not holding back, I rolled my eyes as she rambled on and on. She tried; I gave her credit. But honestly, she didn't have the slightest clue what I liked. The view was probably nice, but trees have never meant anything to me. I wasn't sure why she thought I'd be excited. As we entered the hallway to see the bedrooms, I questioned whether she picked up on my aloofness because she quickly added, "Of course if you'd prefer a different one, we could…"

"The room will be fine, Mom," I interrupted; forcing another smile, knowing full well it wasn't reaching my eyes. Mother, too busy talking about colors and décor, didn't notice, or maybe she did and didn't want to deal with it. It was hard to tell.

Her way of coping was through denial. My entire existence had been that way. Through the help of our group therapy sessions, I thought she had gotten better, but today that all seemed lost. I was afraid she'd slip back into refusing to understand my abilities. That would be her comfort zone—to ignore it completely. I certainly hoped that didn't happen, but without a plan for future sessions, it was a distinct possibility.

When walking into my new bedroom, I came to an immediate halt. This strange mixture of coldness and sadness suddenly caused the hairs on the back of my neck to rise. It was quite an odd sensation, and I didn't want to go in. The desire to peer out the window to see the view my mother hyped about dissipated with my first step. The gray walls increased the uninviting feeling, and I felt like an intruder in my own room. Maybe after the fresh coat of paint Mother kept talking about, and my own furniture, it would start to feel homier.

I half listened as we toured the rest of the house. All I really wanted was to turn around and go back to our home in Clayton. I wasn't trying to be difficult, but since the move was done rather hastily, I'd become skeptical. After coming home from school one day, she announced that we were moving. Just like that, without any warning. Sure, she'd been talking about fresh starts and new beginnings, but I didn't take her seriously. Apparently, I should have.

She was crafty about it, I'd give her that. She set everything up without my knowledge. She got her transfer papers in order for the Veterans Affairs Hospital, which was what brought us to this area, I later learned. They had a position open in the intensive care unit—the same unit she worked—making for a smooth transfer. She had met with a realtor and found this house for a decent price. It had been on the market for ten years, and the owners were desperate to unload it, which was how we ended up in this particular town. My high school papers…everything done behind my back.

The one thing she overlooked, whether intentional or not, was my therapy sessions. She completely failed in finding me a therapist. "We'll have time for that later," was her lame excuse. We scheduled one last session with my therapist, who basically released me from care, and two weeks later, here we were.

Why I was opposed to the move didn't make sense, really. One would think I would be ecstatic to move as far away as possible. There was nothing enjoyable about living in that town. In fact, I hated it. I wasn't even going to miss any friends back there. Truth be known, I didn't have any friends to miss. That was why I was seeing a therapist. It gave me an outlet, someone I could talk openly to about my problem.

The few friends I had, if you could call them friends, turned away from me when I started seeing things. Visions. "Clairvoyant" was the term my therapist used. *Freak* was the term kids at school gave me.

I could understand why they shied away from me, though. We tend to avoid things that were different or odd, and I definitely fell into that category. Even my own mother didn't want any part of it. She certainly wasn't anyone I could confide in. That drove a wedge between us, keeping each other from being particularly close.

Still, it hurt her badly, seeing me treated in that way. But I was all right with it, for the most part. I pulled strength from their pettiness which, in turn, formed me into a stronger person. That lesson taught me to rely on one person, me. That was my solution to things; ignore everyone else and depend on myself. Her solution, though, was to move away from it. I just hoped she wouldn't be disappointed when it started to happen again. No doubt that it would, which was why I was opposed to moving. Back home, at least, they already knew about me. I knew what to expect. I wasn't accepted, by any means, but I knew what to anticipate from their reactions. Here, I didn't have the slightest clue how people would respond. It will drive me crazy, waiting for them to discover my secret.

"So...that's just about it. I know this old house needs a lot of work, but I think with some tender loving care and good old elbow grease, we can turn it into a home...Our home," she said as she panned the room, her eyes glistening over.

Shameful thoughts about my attitude infiltrated my mind as I studied her. While hope filled her eyes, guilt clouded mine. A chance at a normal life was all she wanted for me. Everything she'd done was for my benefit. Caving to my conscience, I stated, "Mom, it's great. I think I'm going to like it here." Much to my own surprise, my sentiment was genuine.

"Aw, Heather..." She came over with her arms spread apart, giving me a hug. "We'll do just fine here." With another squeeze, she eyed the room one last time before saying, "Okay...let's get busy."

Suppressing another sigh, I followed her out to the moving van parked at the end of our driveway, and started the tedious chore of unpacking.

2 Small Steps

The first week of school sucked. All right, it hadn't been all that bad, but if Mother thought it was going to be this perfect fit, and I would instantly make friends, she was sadly mistaken. I'd spent most of my life avoiding close relationships, and I wasn't planning on it being any different here. Regardless, I still felt a twinge of pain when the hopefulness in her eyes quickly shifted to disappointment after she asked how my first few days went.

"Like every other day," was all I contributed before pushing past her and heading straight toward the kitchen. I quickened my steps in a desperate attempt to get away from her. *I did not want to have this conversation.* It was hard enough, knowing I continually disappointed her by my lack of social skills, but she didn't need to continually harp on it.

Opening up the refrigerator door, I reached for the milk carton as Mom's steps sounded behind me. I knew she wasn't going to let the conversation drop that easily, but I was kind of hoping. I just wasn't in the mood to listen to another lecture about making friends. *Would she ever let it go?*

"You know, Heather. You're going to have to put forth a little effort in order for people to be nice to you. It wouldn't hurt for you to at least try," she scolded.

As I poured myself a glass of milk, I stared as the opaque liquid swirled into the glass. *It's easy for her,* I thought. *She doesn't have to worry about being different; she's normal.* I wished more than anything I could be normal like her, and everyone else, but that wasn't reality. Not *my* reality, anyway. In my world, I'd always be a freak. I didn't see that changing. The sooner she realized that, the quicker tension created between us would ease. Honestly, I failed to see the point of trying, because once people discovered the truth, they wouldn't want to know me.

It was obvious by the way she held her hand on her hip, with eyes narrowing in on me, that she wasn't going to let this conversation drop. Deep down I wanted to scream. I needed to change my tactic, otherwise the argument would keep continuing. In my most reassuring voice, I replied, "Don't worry, Mom..., I'll adjust. People aren't backing away from me as I approach them." *Yet,* I mentally added.

"I'm sure, with a small effort, you'll be able to make a friend or two," she countered.

I finally agreed with her to shut down the conversation. She seemed content enough when I told her I would try harder. I didn't actually mean it, but that was what she wanted to hear. Satisfied with my answer, she turned and left the room. Since that was my way out of the argument, I hurried toward my bedroom to escape any further scrutiny. As I shut the door, I closed my eyes, wanting desperately to feel good about being alone. But once I reopened them, the unsettling feeling swept through me again.

I let out a breath as I scanned my room. Even with the walls freshly painted a creamy color, I still couldn't get a sense of coziness there. It certainly didn't feel like home to me. We hadn't lived there for very long, which may be part of the reason, but there was something else. Something I couldn't explain. Aggravated, I shook my head. I might never understand this feeling of displacement whenever I entered this house, but I wanted to figure out why it was strongest in my bedroom. The easiest solution would be to move into a different room. *Would that even make a difference?* I quickly dismissed that notion since it would bring up more questions from Mother. Ones I didn't want to answer.

I dragged myself away from the door and went over to lie down on my bed. As I stared up at the ceiling, I pushed the uneasiness away, and began mulling over what she said. Maybe she's right, and I was just too stubborn to see it her way. I didn't know…It wasn't like I'd tried. I'd been pretty much keeping to myself, like I always did. Maybe I should put forth a little effort. Or at least not recoil when people did reach out to me.

There have been a couple of times people went out of their way for me. I was just polite enough to not be rude, but I immediately went back to my own business, totally ignoring them.

A smile crept across my face as I thought about the guy sitting behind me in my physics class. On my second day of attendance, he went out of his way to make sure I had proper notes from the lesson they were currently on. Right before the teacher arrived to start the lecture, I felt a soft tap on my shoulder. A warm, jolting sensation shot down the side of my arm, causing me to whip around. My eyes grew wider as I took in the sight of him. Staring back at me was the most gorgeous guy I had ever seen. His sandy blond hair was disheveled on top, giving it that just-so-sexy look. But it was his eyes that captivated me in that moment. They were warm and inviting, tinted the softest shade of hazel. I sat there for a second with my mouth slightly ajar as I just stared at him. I was caught completely off guard. Nobody had ever captured my attention that way.

Finally blinking, I couldn't force myself to turn away as the corners of his mouth drew up into a half smirk, obviously aware of my ogling. A warming sensation zinged through my body as the heat crept into my cheeks. I glanced down, embarrassed that he could elicit that type of response. *What the heck was I feeling anyway?*

He waved a stack of papers back and forth as if he was trying to get my attention. Finally, I snapped out of my trance at the realization he was trying to hand them to me. As I snatched the papers, I barely heard him murmur something about notes from the current lesson before turning back around. It was such a nice gesture, especially since I came part way through the lesson, and I was sincerely touched by his kindness. He certainly didn't have to do that. But in that particular moment, I wasn't thinking clearly.

A small chuckle escaped as I remembered my response. Instead of playing it cool or even pretending to be appreciative, all I said in return was a generic thank-you. Then I turned around and discounted him, as if he wasn't important. I didn't even bother with introductions, which I thoroughly regret now, since I still didn't know his name. *Why couldn't I have come up with a proper "thanks?"* I cringed at the thought of him thinking I must be the biggest snob.

No, I certainly hadn't been trying to make friends. Living in my own personal bubble, I think I'd grown accustomed to the contentment. That was where I was most comfortable. I guess I needed to get out of my comfort zone and try. The next time an opportunity like that arises, I was going to make an honest effort. Maybe then Mother would back off. Of course, I probably wouldn't have made that resolution had I known an opportunity would present itself so fast.

As I stepped out of the school's front doors the following day, I heard a male voice yell from behind me. "Heather, wait up, I'll walk with you." Confused as to who would know my name, let alone yell for me, I stopped and slowly turned around. Surprisingly, the guy with the notes from my physics class was jogging to catch up to me. With the sun shining brightly, rays cascading off of him, I inhaled a breath as this gorgeous creature ran toward me. I couldn't do anything else but stare at him. It took a minute for me to collect myself. I knew he was hot when I first noticed him the other day in class, but I had suppressed that thought as quickly as it appeared. I mean, I'd never pined over boys before. *What's the use?* Boyfriends were for other people, not me. But watching him run toward me, unlike all of my previous encounters, I couldn't help but think there was something special about him.

Quickly trying to dismiss lingering thoughts of his hotness level, I was left standing there, wondering why he would want to walk with me. After being indifferent toward him the other day, I found it rather odd he would want anything to do with me. I wanted to run away, but reminded myself about the resolution I made last night, and remained standing. It was hard. It took every ounce of energy I had to fight the urge to escape.

"Hey," he said as he caught up to me. With his half-grin, he extended his hand out offering to shake hands. "Barry," he said as he introduced himself to me. "We haven't officially met."

Mesmerized by his smile, it took me a second to realize what he was doing. Forcing myself to quit staring at his face, I glanced down toward his extended hand. A different type of fear filtered its way through me, filling in all my crevices. A handshake was normally just a polite greeting between two individuals. But he had no way of knowing it caused an overwhelming amount of anxiety deep inside of me. Still staring at his hand, I blurted out, "Heather." Hoping he didn't notice my hesitation, against my better judgment, I went ahead and shook his hand.

Warmth spread throughout my body at his touch, causing me to quickly let go. My anxiety level was at an all-time high, but I tried to appear calm. I was sure I looked like an idiot who had never shaken hands before.

Luckily though, other than throwing a quizzical glance my way, he seemed to discard my erratic behavior. I could imagine what was going through his head, but he certainly didn't act like it fazed him any. "I'm headed in the same direction. You live next to my grandma's house," he clarified. "I saw you move in a few weeks ago."

"Oh..., I haven't met any of my neighbors yet." I stumbled around on my words. Feeling guilty, because I didn't socialize with anyone, I suddenly felt the need to come up with an excuse for not meeting his grandma. "We've been kind of busy, fixing up the house since the move," I added, hoping he bought it. I told myself it wasn't a complete lie since we had been slowly fixing it up.

"Yeah..., that house sat empty for years. Ever since...," Pausing, he winced while running his hands through his hair. It was brief, but sadness overshadowed his face while he hesitated. But he recovered quickly, making me question what I saw. "Well, awhile anyway. Seeing the house occupied again is good." His gaze shifted downward, with a shrug.

"Thanks," I replied, wondering if that was the proper response. Intrigued as to what he was going to say, I wondered how he would've finished the sentence. My curiosity was piqued by his hesitation and peculiar reaction, but I dropped it. Prying into people's business was totally what I wanted to avoid. It was the safest route.

The corners of his lips spread into a shy smile as he looked at me. As we began walking down the sidewalk, I mentally sighed in relief as he steered the conversation toward safer topics. It wasn't long, unfortunately, before he asked the inevitable. "So, what town did you move from?"

The rest of the walk home was spent with us talking about Clayton, the town I came from, as well as the life happenings of this place. Barry was actually pretty cool, easy enough to talk to anyway. I hadn't carried on a conversation that intense with someone my age for a long time. In fact, I didn't even remember the last time I actually had a real conversation with anyone other than my therapist, or Mother.

I must admit, it felt kind of nice. A feeling l had long forgotten.

Keeping the answers about myself kind of vague, he finally touched on the topic I didn't want to discuss, friends. Fabricating a story about them, I pretended it was hard being separated from them, but keeping in touch through the Internet and texting had helped.

That seemed to appease him, but I felt a little guilty lying to him. I was used to telling people what they wanted to hear, I'd done that practically my whole life, but with Barry it didn't feel right for some reason. For the first time in my life, it just felt wrong.

When we arrived at the end of the sidewalk leading up to my front porch, I motioned toward the house. "My exit," I simply said.

Appearing a little unsure, he glanced toward the house while taking a deep breath. As he slowly exhaled, he turned back toward me, staring directly into my eyes. I was unsure what his expression meant. The unsettling declaration in his eyes expressed he wanted to say more, but he remained quiet. After pausing for just a couple of more seconds, he finally said, "Thanks for letting me walk with you. It was nice getting to know you better. Next time, I'll have my car back from the shop and I'll be able to give you a ride." He half grinned, making me catch my breath again. Staring back at him, I seemed to get lost in his entire face. I really didn't understand what, or where, that feeling derived from, but when he smiled like that I couldn't help but want to get to know him better. He was totally hot. I wasn't blind, but it seemed more than just superficial attractiveness. It was a much deeper feeling, more genuine. I hadn't felt like that before.

"I'll hold you to that," I said, smiling back at him despite myself. *Where did that answer come from, and why, all of a sudden, did I have tons of confidence?*

"All right then," he said, grinning. He started to take off for his grandmother's house, but stopped and turned toward me. With a sly grin, he added, "Hey…, I'll look you up during lunch tomorrow, and introduce you to some of my friends."

And with that simple sentence, reality came crashing back. Forcing a smile, I replied, "That would be great." I hoped he didn't pick up on my sudden mood shift, but meeting his friends was the last thing that interested me. I was sure anyone in my position would be elated to have a totally hot guy take his time to make sure they're welcomed, but I felt I'd put forth enough effort for the week. The last thing I wanted to do was pretend to be interested in multiple people.

"Sweet…I'll see you tomorrow." With a little wave, he flashed a quick smile. His eyes drifted toward my house, causing his smile to drop for a second, before they settled back on me. He smiled again, but it was strained. After adjusting his backpack, he turned and headed for his grandma's house.

As I lingered there an extra second, I watched him walk away before heading up my own sidewalk. Slowly, I turned to walk up my stairs, still feeling a bit confused. I liked Barry, that part was pretty clear. He was nice and seemed genuine. Not to mention he was definitely gorgeous. With his tall, slender build, and untidy, sandy-blond hair, he would be on anyone's radar. His perfect jaw-line and those warm, hazel eyes definitely set him apart from other guys. But his smile was completely mesmerizing. The sole problem was me. I wasn't sure if I was ready to become friends with anyone. I'd been solo for a long time and letting people get close scared me. *What if I become friends with people here and then my visions start again?* It would be just like the last time all over again minus the actual having friends part.

Doubt began to sink in quickly as I thought maybe it would be best to keep a safe distance. Besides, with one school year left anyway, what was the point of even trying? Quickly talking myself out of meeting his friends tomorrow, I snapped to the present.

Before tomorrow could happen, I would have to face my next step, Mother. She was home because I noticed her car parked in the driveway. I was sure she saw me walking beside Barry, which probably raised her interest. I groaned inwardly as I headed inside for the interrogation I knew would begin.

3 The Toy

"I'm home," I yelled as I walked through the doorway. The entryway mirror caught my reflection, making me pause as I stood there staring. I tilted my head to the side as I studied a little deeper, wondering what I was getting worked up about. There wasn't any way he'd find me attractive because I was just like every other girl. The one thing separating me from all of the other girls who sported long brown hair was the hint of red highlights that's naturally sprinkled throughout mine. My eyes were darker brown than most, about the color of espresso, but other than that, there wasn't anything special about me.

"In here, honey. Can you hold these curtains while I drape them around the rod?"

"Just a sec," I answered as I glanced one more time at my reflection. Knowing there wasn't anything I could do to change my appearance; I scrunched my face into a goofy pose before childishly sticking my tongue out. I'd never cared about my appearance before, and I wasn't going to start now. Determined to stop worrying about it, I walked into the living room to help Mom. As I dropped my book bag down on the couch, my thoughts kept drifting back to Barry. Mentally replaying him running toward me brought an unmistakable warming sensation deep in my chest. My cheeks flushed at the memory of the sun cascading off his tanned body, causing a small smile to escape. I didn't understand what that meant, but I found myself conflicted. Maybe it wasn't such a bad idea to meet some of his friends. After all, it was the part of my resolution that I had to keep reminding myself about.

As if reading my mind, Mom tried keeping her tone even as she asked, "Who was that guy you were walking with?" She didn't do a very good job at being nonchalant because her voice was laced with curiosity.

I audibly sighed before replying. "Barry. He's in my physics class. His car is being worked on, so he walked home with me since he was going to his grandma's house. I guess she lives right next door to us."

"Oh, that's nice," she stated, still trying to appear indifferent. But I could imagine the wheels turning in her head and sense her pleasure at the sight of me talking to someone. "Maybe he can introduce you to some of his friends."

"One step ahead of you, Mom. He told me he would tomorrow at school." I concentrated on the fabric in my hand, wishing she would drop the subject. I hated discussing friends with Mother since she desperately wanted me to have them. Yet the outcome was always the same—disappointment.

"That's great. It's just what you need," she stated confidently. With the content expression she wore, I was sure she thought we'd already benefited from the move. Who knows, maybe we had, and I was just too stubborn to admit it.

Wanting to retreat to my bedroom, I handed her the last part of the drapery and started walking away. When I went to pick up my book bag, I noticed a faded blue toy truck lying harmlessly against my bag. *How odd.* Curious as to what it was doing here, I asked, "What's with the toy truck?"

"Oh, I found it while cleaning out the hallway closet. It's kind of cute, but well used. I thought about bringing it to work to see if somebody's child would want it, but I'm afraid the condition is too rough. I'll probably just throw it out."

Intrigued, I bent down to inspect it closer. Mom was right; it had been played with a lot. By the way the toy was banged-up; the child must have really enjoyed playing with it. Further examining the dents and scratches, I decided they were placed there by some little boy's passion for his toys. I couldn't help but smile as I thought of old Pinchers. Pinchers was a stuffed lobster that I had carried everywhere with me. Where I went, Pinchers went. I would have been devastated to have moved out of my house then later realized Pinchers was left behind.

I didn't know why but either out of curiosity, or just plain stupidity, I reached down to pick up the truck. As soon as my fingers grabbed a hold of the banged-up metal, a picture of a little boy around seven years old flashed through my mind. He was outside playing, smiling up at me. His smiles turned quickly into tears as a wave of sadness and fear overcame my body.

I dropped the toy as if it was on fire and inhaled a deep breath. As I stood completely still, I tried blocking out what I had witnessed. My plan was futile, for I knew it was too late. The vision had already been planted.

"What's the matter?" Mom asked apprehensively, all her confidence from earlier quickly fading away as her stare bored into my back.

"Nothing," I replied, trying to sound reassuring, but my voice was shaky, giving away my lack of composure. With my back still to her, she couldn't see my expression, but she knew anyway. She wasn't stupid. "I'm going outside for a minute," I stated, not waiting for her to answer as I snatched up my handbag and hurried toward the backdoor.

Once I was out of sight, I picked up speed and ran out into the woods behind our house. I wasn't sure where I was going, as I'd never been in these woods before, but it seemed like a good refuge. At least a far enough distance away from what I had just seen. The briar branches were whipping past me, scratching my skin, and snagging at my shirt as I went, but I didn't care. I just kept running and running, trying not to trip over the roots sticking up from the ground, until I came upon a ravine.

As I slowed to a stop, I bent over, and rested my hands on my knees for support as I breathed heavily. The woods were completely deserted, and I could hear the barking sounds of the squirrels playing nearby. I was instantly jealous of how innocent they sounded. *Why couldn't my life be that carefree?*

I squeezed my eyes shut, while clenching my fists, wanting nothing more than to scream at the life I'd been dealt. I needed to release my sudden anger, so I pressed clenched hands into my thighs in hopes of calming myself down. When part of the tension gradually released, my shoulders slouched while standing back up. The anger had lessened some, allotting me better control over my emotions. With a few labored breaths, I scanned the surrounding area. Off to my left, I saw a log that had fallen near a neighboring tree. The way they were wedged against each other created an ideal bench. Without thinking, I automatically went over and sat down. The rough bark felt moist underneath my hands, but I didn't care. I needed to rest. My hands were trembling as I fidgeted around my bag until finally coming across my pack of cigarettes. A nasty habit I wanted to stop, but times like these were why I kept reaching for them. Finally managing to extract one and light it, I took a puff.

Afraid of closing my eyes, I stared straight ahead into the woods. Small streaks of sunlight shone through the trees, making everything seem golden and crisp. Despite the beautiful scenery surrounding me, the image of the boy remained in my head, tarnishing the beauty. A humorless laugh escaped as I wondered why I feared closing them. It didn't matter if my eyes were closed or not, I could still visualize him. And I knew his fate. I may not know the exact circumstances, but I already knew his life had ended horribly.

KIMBERLY READNOUR

Deflated, I laid my head against the tree I was leaning on. *Why did I touch that toy?* I knew better. That was all it took, a simple touch, which was why I was hesitant to shake Barry's hand. I didn't want to take the risk of him seeing me during one of my visions. Luckily nothing happened when our hands touched, but I fear in time someone will find out. Then, I fear it will be just like Clayton all over again.

That simple touch was how people found out my secret, back home. While walking down the hallway a girl, Kelsey, had come up behind me. All she wanted was the notes from the last hour, a simple request, I thought. After she was through, she thanked me but reached over touching my arm at the same time. As soon as she did this, her shirt came in contact with my bare skin. Except it wasn't her own shirt she was wearing. It originally belonged to April, her best friend, who'd been missing for a month.

The vision came at me strongly. It was like I became April, feeling her anxiety as she woke up with the realization she'd been kidnapped. I stood there in front of Kelsey with a very dazed and frightened expression upon my face. I remember feeling very groggy and cold as I visualized gazing out a tiny window. The window was the key to her location. The lake and a few other distinguishing features displayed through the glass panes provided enough clues for the police to find her. Toward the end of the vision, total fear had engulfed me, as her killer came toward her…I screamed a blood-curdling scream, reliving what April had experienced. Everyone who was in the hallway with me and Kelsey had stood there watching with horror-stricken faces.

I took another puff trying desperately to shake off that memory. No, I didn't want people at this school witnessing me going through another vision, especially one of that magnitude. I was sure this town wouldn't react any differently than the people from Clayton. Those smaller towns were usually all the same.

Finally surrendering to my exhaustion, or maybe just frustration, I closed my eyes. While resting for a minute, I heard a quick rustling sound, like someone running past. My eyes automatically popped open as I quickly scanned the area. Nothing had changed.

Confused, I called out, "Who's there?" while trying to find the source behind the sound I heard. "Show yourself," I demanded, but there was nothing but silence. Beginning to think I was acting completely foolish, I got up to head back home. As I started to leave, I glanced over my shoulder, still questioning where the sound generated. I shivered as a chilling sensation ran down my spine, and I couldn't shake the eerie feeling that I wasn't alone.

4 Nightmares

"What did you get on the physics quiz?" Barry asked as he walked me out of class.

"I didn't do too well, an eighty-eight," I said, kind of embarrassed. My grades have always been this side of decent, but they weren't anywhere near the high honor level.

"That's not too bad. I got a ninety-two, which I'm definitely all right with." While running his fingers through his sandy blond hair, he asked, "Hey, I'm going to my grandma's house after school today. Do you want a lift?"

"Sure. Meet you outside after school?"

"Okay..." He smiled as his body seemed to relax. With a quick wave, he turned and walked down the hallway.

I stood there watching him until he turned the corner and disappeared out of sight before turning into my own classroom. His smile was going to be my undoing. As I took my seat, I barely heard the teacher begin—I was lost in thought. I kept mulling over Barry and my latest vision. With everything that had happened to me this past week, concentrating on the lecture was difficult.

Actually, the week had been going well, all things considered. After returning from the woods the other day, I started searching for the toy truck. Not fooling Mom when I hastily departed, she had it hidden before I returned. She hesitated when I asked where it was, making me wonder if she'd answer. After a few seconds, she glanced over toward me, questioning if she should dispose of it. My instincts wanted to say yes...get that thing as far away as possible, but my mind recognized the importance. She gave me a disapproving look when I told her we'd better hang on to it a little longer. She was displeased, but she agreed to keep it, which surprised me. That was exactly what I feared, Mother being disappointed when a vision occurred. Honestly, I didn't think it would happen that soon.

The young boy had been haunting my dreams every night since I touched that toy. Knowing he could invade my nightly sanctuary that easily was unsettling, if not disturbing. There wasn't any peace to myself anymore. Never having dreamt about any of my visions, I didn't know what to think. Ever since the vision occurred, something different had been going on, because he consumed my life. Even when I let myself think about Barry—which I found myself doing more than I'd like to admit—my thoughts strayed back to that little boy. For some reason, my mind intertwined them, disallowing me to think of one without the other. It was strange.

But the child wanted something from me, and I kept wondering what it could be. Sometimes, when those dreams occurred, I woke up with an inkling that he was trying to communicate with me. Unable to figure it out was slowly driving me crazy.

Each dream started out the same, he was happy, playing in his backyard, then turned to face me. His expression seemed one of recognition, but then it flashed forward to tears running down his face. Before I wake up; however, he appeared to be opening his mouth to tell me something, but I never hear what he tried to say. Unable to fall back asleep, I lay there unsuccessfully trying to figure it out.

Finally I had to push those thoughts out of my head as I sat in class, clearly not listening to the teacher. As Mrs. Pickard went over the first battle of the civil war, I sat there numb. All I really wanted was to go home and end this charade, not hear about Fort Sumter. Part of me felt bad for feeling that way since Barry had been an enormous help. He definitely made my transition into this school tolerable. And I almost felt half-way normal around everyone…Almost.

As promised, he introduced me to his friends during lunch a couple of days back—all five of them. When we met in the lunchroom and walked toward an awaiting table, I wanted to turn back around. In my mind, I pictured a few other people, not a crowd, but it turned out all right. Everyone seemed nice enough, polite even, but I didn't feel completely relaxed around them yet. I was like an outsider, peering through a window at a group of people who were clearly at ease with each other. I supposed that would be normal, since I was new, but it will take me awhile to get used to them.

I'd forgotten most of their names, except for Caleb and Nicole. Caleb was easy to remember since he kept including me in their conversations—or at least he tried. Plus he liked to tease Barry. Watching the way they bantered back and forth with each other, I assumed they were best friends. The way Barry interacted with everyone made me realize exactly what I'd been missing.

Nicole's the only girl in the group. She was rather quiet at lunch, but since then had been going out of her way to talk to me. She was actually in a few of my classes, which made it easier to get to know her. As time goes by maybe I'd be comfortable enough around her to start initiating conversations. Honestly though, I didn't see myself ever reaching that level of closeness with anyone. Especially forming the bonds best friends have since I never fully open myself up to anyone. I felt trapped, constantly holding part of myself back, while the fear that something would trigger my ability lays dormant waiting to surface. That apprehension continued to linger over me the entire time I engaged in conversation. Well, with everyone except Barry.

The last bell of the day rang, pulling me out of my thoughts. I gathered up my belongings, went to my locker to grab what I needed, and made a quick dash outside to meet Barry.

"You ready to go?" he asked with his big smile. That was another quality I liked about him, he always appeared happy. That trait was so different from my life, it almost seemed foreign. I certainly hadn't been familiar with any happiness, especially that past year. I found it rather refreshing.

"Yes, sir," I replied, following him out to his car. It still surprised me how at ease I felt around him. When I was with him, I could be myself, and not have to pretend to appease him. I had to be careful, though. If I become too relaxed, my ability might resurface, causing him to slip away from me as easily as he came.

"So, you're going to your grandma's on a Friday night?" I asked out of curiosity.

He laughed. "I know, sounds weird. Grandma's like another mom to me, though. Since my mom's a single parent, Grandma practically raised me. I like keeping her company at least one night during the weekend."

"That's really nice, Barry. Not too many people would do that."

As I turned to view him, I noticed that his lips were turned upward in a small grin. *He's cute*, I thought, continuing to stare at him. It was that exact moment when I realized how attracted I was to him. Not only am I captivated by his good genetics, but his personality as well. He had a certain charm to him that drew me in. For the first time in my life, I'd become close enough with someone to generate feelings for them. At least close enough to care, something I didn't see coming at all. I was a little surprised at my revelation, but it didn't stop me from admiring him.

"What?" he asked quizzically.

"Nothing." I quickly turned away, embarrassed to be caught ogling again. His tiny grin grew into a large smile, making me think he didn't mind my gawking. But still, I needed to get better control of my actions.

After pulling up into his grandma's drive, he turned toward me. "Hey, are you busy later on? I'd like you to come over and meet Grandma. I know she'd like to meet you, too. You know, neighbors and all." He playfully jabbed me in my side. "Afterward, we could watch a movie or something."

With an eyebrow cocked, I peered up at him, asking suspiciously, "A date…? At your grandma's house?"

"Um, yeah…It sounds kind of lame when you put it that way." He laughed. "Say yes, and I promise I'll make it up to you later."

"That sounds good. I can probably come over around six o'clock," I replied a little too fast, still surprised how easy it was to talk to him.

"Great. I'll see you then," he said as we got out of his car.

As I walked home, that familiar warmth swelled through me. The sensations were rather enjoyable. It occurred to me—I was actually looking forward to something, and…happy. For the first time in over a year, I opened my front door wearing a smile on my face.

5 Exposed

When walking over to meet Barry, I had to laugh. The thought of Mom's reaction when I told her I was coming over here was comical. I'd never seen her that giddy. She was so elated, I thought she'd burst. All through supper she couldn't wipe the smile off her face, but what got to me were her eyes. They sparkled so brightly, at first, I was glad to be the reason behind their shine. But sadness slowly crept in when I realized going to a friend's house shouldn't elicit that type of reaction. It was a stark reminder of how isolated I'd become.

I knew she meant well, but part of me couldn't wait to get away from her. There was a limit on how much I could take of her constant babble, and since she was in overdrive tonight, I had my fill. Judging from her smug expression, I could tell she thought moving here was the best thing she'd ever done for me. She stopped short of saying it, but it was written all over her face. Who knows? A part of me was beginning to think she might be right after all.

When stepping onto the landing leading to his grandma's front porch, all thoughts of Mother were erased. Anxiety replaced it, swirling around in the pit of my stomach. *Would it be a smart idea to spend an entire evening with someone?* Wanting to retreat, I didn't feel as brave as I did just seconds before stepping onto the concrete. In a desperate attempt to not chicken out I took a deep breath, hoping to relax my nerves. Slowly exhaling, I squeezed my eyes closed as I rang the doorbell.

To my surprise the door swung swiftly open, making me wonder for a second if he had been waiting right by it. "Hey. Come on in." Barry greeted me with that big smile of his, the one I'd grown to adore. "Grandma's in the kitchen finishing up the dishes." He motioned down a narrow hallway, which I presumed led to the kitchen. "Follow me." He cocked his head, turning to allow me to follow him down the narrow path.

I immediately felt welcomed as we stepped into the living room, and my anxiety disappeared as quickly as it came. The house had a warm, cozy, inviting feeling. As I followed Barry, I quickly scanned the area. The sofa was older, golden in color, with actual doilies covering the armrests. Quite typical, it seemed, for someone her age, having lived in the same house for many years. An old rattan rocking chair was by the couch, with a worn but snuggly looking afghan draped over it. Many pictures of Barry lined the outdated, papered walls.

As we approached the kitchen, the scent of vanilla and chocolate hit me, and my stomach immediately growled. As we rounded the corner I saw the culprit, a plate full of freshly baked chocolate chip cookies sitting on the kitchen table.

"Are you hungry?" Barry asked as he grinned.

Embarrassed that he heard my stomach, I blushed. "No, I just got done eating supper."

His grin grew wider as he cocked his head toward me, whispering, "Grandma has snacks. She always has snacks."

Much to my surprise, meeting his grandma was especially nice. She was the perfect stereotypical grandma, like the ones I'd pictured from the fifties. White hair fixed in a bun, heavy set, the constantly making a fuss over you type. She was exactly the kind I'd always dreamt of if my grandmother had still been alive. I wasn't sure I'd ever met anyone quite like her before. No wonder Barry liked coming here, who wouldn't? She spoiled you completely.

After refusing our offer to help dry the dishes, she shooed us back into the living room. "Now, you kids just go watch your movie. I'll pop you some popcorn and bring it out to you shortly," she said as she practically threw us out of the kitchen.

Grabbing the drinks she handed me, I followed Barry—who had snatched up the plate of cookies—back toward the living room. Once we entered the room, I hesitated for a second. That same tingling in the pit of my stomach returned as I scoped the seating arrangements. My mouth felt dry, like it was going to close off, and I swallowed hard. The drinks in my hand suddenly seemed very appealing, but I was too frozen to take a sip. I knew why I had unexpectedly felt that apprehension. I was concerned as to where I was going to sit. Quickly sizing up the situation, the rocker appeared too uncomfortable, which really left the couch as the most feasible place. That would mean I would have to sit right next to him, which unexpectedly caused a spark to ignite deep down inside me. Placing the plate of cookies down on the coffee table, Barry turned to grab the drinks from me. Unable to look him in the eye, I nervously handed them over.

"Have a seat," he said, while motioning his arms toward the couch, fortunately making the decision a little easier for me.

I smiled shyly as I sat down. *Why am I anxious to be sitting by him?* I'd been close to him many times that past week in the car and in the cafeteria during lunch, but here at his grandmother's house it just seemed more intimate. I was really starting to stress out about it.

My past problems a forgotten memory, all I could seem to focus on was wondering if he returned the same apprehension. But my anxiety confused me because there was an underlying attraction attached to it. Not once in my entire life had I ever worried about a boy, or what they thought about me. That nervousness was so unfamiliar that I couldn't get used to it. I knew for sure I didn't like it. Or I did. I was too indecisive.

As he edged his way over toward me, my pulse quickened at the realization he was going to sit down next to me. Right next to me, and I couldn't believe how much pleasure that simple action sparked. It was stupid to feel that way. He was only sitting by me, for crying out loud. My gaze shifted toward him as he moved to get back up and reached for the afghan.

Smiling warmly at me, he said, "Here, I thought we could share the blanket."

I really wasn't cold, but I wasn't going to pass up the opportunity of sharing a blanket with him. The idea of us being that close together caused another flutter in my stomach. *Besides,* I thought, *what could go wrong?* As he draped it over us, the blanket descended on top of me, immediately causing me to go rigid. As my body stiffened, my face lost all expression as the image of the boy, the boy that had been haunting my dreams, flashed across my mind...*This time he was happy and giggling all bundled up. "All right Johnny, you can watch the cartoons before your nap." As quickly as that endearing scene played out, a feeling of anguish hastily replaced any contentment I had as he sat, crying...Not a normal cry that children often do, but one of fear. Great sadness overshadowed me as he called out, "I want my mommy"...Then finally horror...Pure horror engulfed my body as I began to break out in a sweat. Small flashes of the guy...the killer...dark hair, I could barely make out his face when suddenly I saw his eyes...*

With a sharp intake of air, I gasped, whispering to myself, "Johnny" as my hands trembled. I sat still for a second, trying to dismiss the image out of my mind, while my breath caught back up to me. As my eyes began to focus on the present, I glanced toward Barry. Much to my horror, I saw him staring wide eyed at me as if I was a...freak. I was mortified that I had a vision right in front of him.

All my chances of having a normal relationship with someone quickly evaporated away as the reality of who I truly am came crashing down around me. As devastated as I was at losing the one shot at a decent relationship, I couldn't worry about myself right now. I had to think of the little boy. The vision, what made it come? When I glanced down, the afghan had slid off, lying sinisterly on the floor. I scurried away from it as if it were a snake, peering back toward Barry.

"Johnny...the boy's name was Johnny. Who's Johnny?" I demanded, not really expecting him to respond. But I was desperate—desperate for answers.

Still staring at me, I was unable to read his expression. His face was contorted, but didn't appear to be completely disgusted. Instead, there was a sense of confusion, along with a hint of sadness. I remained still, contemplating what could be going through his mind. Surprise, of course, but he had such an underlining look of sorrow that I couldn't quite understand. Swallowing hard, he barely whispered, "Johnny lived next door. In the house you're living in now."

It all began to fall into place, the toy—my dreams. More pieces of the puzzle revealed, with edges that are actually starting to snap together. I laughed sarcastically. It was ironic...Mom moved me four hundred miles away to try to dispel my visions only to lead me right in the middle of another one. *Why? Of all places to live, why did she have to pick that house? Was there no place safe?*

I wanted to scream.

"How did you...? What just happened?"

Wanting my own questions answered first, I ignored his quick interrogation. I glanced downward at the afghan, and then asked the obvious, "Did he used to come over here?"

"My grandma babysat for him," he said slowly, still observing me suspiciously.

"The afghan…He used to cuddle up in it. How long ago did he die?"

He kept staring at me, clearly not understanding what was going on yet. I realized he deserved answers, too, but I needed to find out a few more details to put my own mind at ease. I sat there anxiously waiting for him to process everything in order to speak again.

After a few minutes, he answered in a gravelly voice, "He went missing ten years ago. I… I guess one would presume he's dead, but they never found his body." Sadness quickly filled his eyes, and I wanted to erase the pain I'd resurrected.

"You knew him quite well," I stated in a more compassionate tone.

"He was my friend. He's our age you know, or at least would have been. I played with him every time I came over here, which was a lot."

There wasn't any sparkle left in Barry's eyes, and I could tell this was a very difficult topic for him to discuss. The pain that lined his face was too much for me to bear. Seeing him in this depressed state made me want to reach out to him, to hold him, but I didn't dare. By now, I was sure he was afraid of me, thinking that I was the biggest freak that ever entered his life.

"I see visions," I blurted out. As soon as the words sprang out of my mouth, I immediately wanted to take them back.

"What?" he asked. I studied him for a second. There was just enough tenderness paired with a hint of curiosity in his eyes that actually made me feel comfortable enough to continue talking.

Though still not confident enough to make direct eye contact with him, I stared down toward the floor, fidgeting with my fingers. "I can see things, visions. If I touch something that belonged to someone, something they treasured, or meant something to them, sometimes I get a vision about them." I glanced over at the afghan before forcing myself to look at him.

Half afraid of what I might see—like a horrified expression and him whipping out a crucifix—he was still staring at me wide eyed, but the shocked expression of earlier was replaced with general concern. He must have understood what my words meant, to a certain level, because he quickly gathered the blanket and threw it back toward the rocking chair.

"Do you mean you can see and hear them…like a movie playing?"

"Sort of," I said. Then it occurred to me, I *was* able to hear something. Before it had solely been things I saw and felt, but this time I actually heard voices…"I saw him wrapped up in the afghan, and then I heard…" Pausing, I glanced toward the kitchen for a second. Returning my eyes toward Barry, I swallowed before continuing. "I heard your grandmother's voice say his name." Hearing myself admit that out loud threw me off for a moment.

Then my adrenaline took over and I couldn't help but get excited about my newfound level of discovery. It took all my strength to suppress my emotions for I knew this wasn't the time to show excitement. "That's how I knew his name," I whispered more to myself.

"That's incredible," he softly spoke, matching my tone. "So it's happened before?"

At that very moment, the hint of excitement I felt swiftly drained from my body as I recollected my memories. Staring down again, I sighed heavily before admitting, "Yes, back in my hometown. That's the real reason my mom moved us here. Let's just say, nobody there *appreciated* my gift."

Slowly, I raised my eyes back to him, not knowing quite what to expect. Staring inquisitively back at me, he opened his mouth as if to say something, but stopped. He paused for a second, I presumed to recollect his thoughts before finally asking, "May I ask what happened?"

When explaining the vision I had about April, I half expected him to start running away, or at least ask me to leave. He did neither. Instead, he listened quietly as I explained her murder, what led me to seeing her, and the shocking conclusion of who her murderer turned out to be. It was hard reliving the vision for him, and embarrassing, having to explain people's reaction toward me afterward.

"So… After I explained the lake setting and the lighthouse to the police, it was enough information to lead them to her whereabouts. Unfortunately, it was too late, she had already been killed." Letting out a sigh, I smirked. "The one positive spin was the police collected enough evidence to convict him."

A shiver ran through my body as I recollected his face. I think that was the worst part, those murderous faces haunt me like pictures refusing to fade away.

"Weren't her parents at least appreciative of you for leading the police to her murderer?"

"You'd think, right?" I deadpanned. "I truly believe over time they will realize, but for now they blame me for not coming forward sooner. They think I could have saved her if I had seen it earlier. But it doesn't work that way for me. I have to touch something that belonged to the victim. I didn't even know the full extent of my ability until I had come in contact with her sweater. Had I known, I would have gladly helped out sooner." My voice cracked at the end, causing me to shut my eyes. I didn't want to chance Barry seeing them glistening up.

He reached over and squeezed my arm. My eyes sprung open, gaping at him with a mixture of surprise and wonderment. Nobody dared to touch me after finding out what I can do—nobody. People steered clear of me at my old school as if I had the plague.

I think my feelings for Barry grew at a deeper level from just that simple touch. Finally realizing what he had done, he let up on the pressure. Instead of letting go, like I thought he would, he slid his fingers down my arm and grabbed a hold of my hand. I sat there dazed, afraid to move for if I moved he'd realize what I am and never touch me again.

While staring intently he said, "Heather, you did nothing wrong. Every person out there who judged you are the ones who are wrong. What you're capable of doing is remarkable—a gift to be treasured, not cursed. You just need to channel it toward the good." I turned away, shaking my head, but he touched my face softly, turning it back toward him. Tingles ran down my neck as warmth began to spread. Still holding my gaze, I couldn't breathe as I got lost in the depths of green-speckled honey tones. Speaking softly, he added, "You need to believe me. They had no right to judge you that way."

His assessment brought me out of my stupor, as I answered, "I...I guess you're right, but I always feel guilty. What if I had seen the vision sooner? They may have rescued her instead of finding her body in that..."

"Maybe, but you don't know that." He interrupted me and then countered. "And besides, you simply can't live that way. Now that you're aware of your capabilities, if the situation ever arises again, you'll know what to do. Until then, you have to live in the present. And, if you hadn't seen the vision, she would still be missing, and a killer would still be roaming the streets. Or worse yet, still be working at the school, searching for his next prey."

Not once, in all my therapy sessions, did that angle ever occur to me. The surrounding air lightened as his simple words lifted the guilt weighing me down. My conscience may not be clear, but the pressure had diminished at least. Tears welled up in my eyes again, but this time I didn't care if he saw. "Thanks." I managed to squeak out.

"You're welcome. Do you think you can help Johnny?" he asked tenderly. Although he still appeared apprehensive, there seemed to be an odd sense of hope in his eyes.

"I don't know, but I'm going to try. My gut instinct tells me it needs to be done. It will help to know a few more facts."

"I'll definitely help if you want. I don't like the idea of you being alone when the visions occur. They seem scary."

I sat in disbelief from the amount of sincerity pouring from his face. His unwavering self-control amazed me, but offering to help...? That was beyond shocking. And it wasn't an act either, he honestly wanted to.

Not knowing quite how to respond, I just nodded. Barry surprised me on so many levels that I was beginning to believe he truly was a great guy.

6 Revelations

While standing in my kitchen, the argument with my mother was wearing on me. I turned so I wouldn't have to face her anymore, hoping that would encourage her to be quiet. My plan backfired; however, as that seemed to heighten her relentless nagging. As I stood motionless, waiting for her rant to be finished, I stared out the back door screen, watching the raindrops fall gently to the ground.

Bit by bit, I began to tune her out as my mind started drifting toward the picturesque view in front of me. The green foliage mixed in with splashes of brown hues was rather refreshing. I found that strange because I'd never cared about forest scenes before. They're trees, for crying out loud. But for some reason, these particular woods had an allure that made me want to run into them and escape. Maybe find the fallen log I claimed as my personal refuge spot from the other day. As the trees swayed from the light breeze, I sighed at the thought. Of course, anything sounded better than quarreling with my mother.

"Mom, I need the truck. Please…just go get it." I begged as soon as I realized she had stopped talking. My voice, clearly frustrated, sounded exhausted. And I was tired of many things, including this argument.

"Fine…" Throwing her hands up in defeat, she reluctantly agreed. "I don't understand why you want to torture yourself," she mumbled as she left the room.

I hated arguing with her because she'd never be able to understand. *Why even try to explain since she doesn't listen?* She only wanted to hear positive things, not reality. Well, not my reality anyway. Frustrated, I scanned the counter noticing my bag lying there. Quickly snatching it up, I stormed out the backdoor letting it slam behind me. After plopping down on the top step, I sat there for a minute staring off into the woods as they continued to entice me.

The rain tapered into a slight drizzle, making everything wet and refreshing. When I inhaled deeply, the earthly scent heightened my awareness, tempting me to run away from here as fast as my legs could carry me. Unfortunately, I couldn't go anywhere until I made Mother understand my need for the truck.

How can I make her understand without frightening her? The boy, Johnny, haunts my dreams every night. If she knew this, she'd get it, but knowing would upset her. *What should I do?*

The entire situation was crazy. She wouldn't handle knowing my dreams were being invaded. No...The best way, for now, was to remain quiet, and let her think I was being difficult.

Johnny's disappearance had taken its toll on Barry and his grandmother. They were very close to him, and in a sense had lost a family member. As Barry shared his memories, it was obvious that had been a dark period for them. Barry told me his grandmother used to sit and peer out her window toward my house while silently praying.

The pain everyone endured during that time was unthinkable.

Johnny went missing on a Saturday while playing in his backyard, which coincided with the vision. The police searched for several months, but without any clues, the case went cold. Although I had a hunch he knew his killer, I needed to have another vision to confirm. I stopped Barry from telling me anymore because I didn't want to cloud any future visions.

After we stopped talking about Johnny last night, the mood was too heavy to focus on the movie...at least for me anyway. The little boy was all I could think about, and how to help him. Part of that help was going forward with another vision, which was why Barry's coming over later. It was crucial I get the truck because he'd be here in a couple of hours.

While reaching for my pack of cigarettes, I let out a frustrated moan. I just wanted to put an end to this craziness. As I pulled a single stick out and started to light it, I heard a noise sounding like feet fast approaching. My head jerked to the left, thinking Barry had come early. All I saw was an empty yard. I stilled in hopes of hearing it again, but nothing out of the ordinary happened. The barking of a neighbor's dog, along with a diesel truck roaring to life, sounded in the distance. The soft patter of raindrops hitting the ground was the one other noise. Finally dismissing it as nothing more than the wind, I lit my cigarette. As I inhaled a puff, I wondered if my nerves were playing tricks with my brain. I was anxious since Barry would be with me while I try having another vision.

I was grateful for his help. He'd be able to decipher part of the clues since he was familiar with the case. But at the same time, I was apprehensive about having another vision in front of him. *What if I do something that totally freaks him out?* I could only hope he could handle it. Deep down, I knew it was the right thing, but my vulnerability weighed heavily on me.

Should I trust him? My thoughts conflicted with my actions as I questioned what I was obviously going to do.

Another point to consider was talking to the police. Eventually, I was going to have to get them involved, but I couldn't yet. It was too soon. I have nothing to contribute, other than the fact that I had a couple of visions and consistent dreams. Maybe after this next vision, I'd have more information that could be useful.

"Heather, I put the truck on your desk in your bedroom," Mother said, bringing me back to the present. "I understand the need for going through with this. I do. If there's a slight chance of you helping, then I suppose it's for the best. But you're my daughter. I hate seeing the harm inflicted on you, so I think it's best if I leave. There are several errands I need to do, so I'll be gone awhile."

After a long pause, she raised her voice adding, "And you really need to quit smoking."

My jaw clamped shut, preventing regrettable words from escaping. As I smashed the cigarette into the concrete, twisting it back and forth, I managed to say, "Thanks, Mom." Not turning around to look at her, I continued staring straight ahead. A couple of moments passed before she turned around and left without saying another word.

After sitting there a couple of minutes, the magnetic attraction of the woods was too powerful for me to resist. Funny how there was a strong sensation of familiarity with the woods, when in truth I'd been there only once. Whenever I stared out into the landscaping, that odd sense of belonging was always present. I smirked, thinking that a bunch of trees that held no meaning to me were now my sanctuary.

Oh, the irony.

As I walked along the imaginary path carved in my mind, I brushed aside the branches from the saplings that grew everywhere. I kept replaying the argument with my mother as I continued pressing forward. The pressure was easy enough to handle, I guess, but I wished she'd let up. The last thing I wanted to do was start up therapy sessions, but it had been the most successful way to communicate.

By the time I stumbled across my familiar log, I was deep in thought. Briefly wondering how I found the area, a hint of a smile crossed my face when a strange sense of reprieve rushed through me. Without further thought, I went straight over and sat. As I ran my hands along the rough bark, I bit my lower lip when my palms became tacky from the damp wood. Quickly dismissing the worry about my clothes getting wet or ruined, I curled up into a ball against the tree. It was confusing as to where the contentment came from, because the last time I sat there was unnerving. The reason might have been unclear, but I was definitely affected by these woods.

As I took in my surroundings, I thought how quiet it was out here. *Could that be the reason?* I needed this serenity to balance my crazy life? I took a deep breath before closing my eyes for a second. While releasing the negative feelings about Mother, my thoughts shifted to my current dreams. Last night was a little different. It started out the same as the rest, but it ended differently. As he opened his mouth to speak, the word *woods* rang through my head before I woke rather abruptly. It seemed these woods played a significant role, which started shaping the corner pieces of my imaginary puzzle. The entire picture had yet to be figured out, stressing the importance of finding out what happened to him.

The longer I sat, the more my body relaxed. I tried to fight the effects of my lack of sleep, but even the cold dampness wasn't enough to keep me awake, and soon I drifted off.

A noise sent a jolt of adrenaline racing through me as my eyes popped open, sharply turning toward my right. The drowsiness of just a few seconds ago became a distant memory. The noise was unmistakable, a little kid laughing. I saw something too. A small shadowy figure ran by and then vanished, but nobody was there. Trying to come up with a rationalization, I thought perhaps my eyes were blurry from opening them quickly.

"Johnny?" I called, feeling foolish as the words flew out. *How could it be him?* I sat there for a second, holding my breath, desperate to hear that noise again, but silence surrounded me.

I walked over to where I saw the shadowy figure dissipate, hoping to find some animal or something that made sense. Once I got there, the only thing to be seen was the tall, brown bark of the trees. Mixed in the picture were a few wild flowers and dried leaves blanketing the ground, freakishly undisturbed. That alone was unnerving. I thought perhaps whatever it was had run down the ravine, so I scooted toward the edge to peer over. As I approached, disappointment set in. The slope, filled with thick patches of briars, made it impossible for any human to tackle. I began to wonder if I was starting to imagine things and decided to head back toward my house.

As I started walking out, that same chilling sensation I felt earlier in the week ran down my spine. I shifted my eyes sideways before picking up my pace, anxious to get home and be with Barry.

7 Secrets

"Are you sure about this?" Barry asked. While trying to disguise his apprehension, the tiny lines creasing his forehead striped with worry.

"Yeah, I have to."

What a pair we made—trying to act as though we're tough while hiding our own insecurities. Although trying my hardest at sounding casual, my shaky voice had to alert him to my apprehension. Not recovered from being in the woods, the hot shower and change of clothes did little to calm me.

"I'm hoping we can find something out too, but I'm more concerned about the toll it takes on you. Are you sure you'll be okay?"

Barry's concern for my welfare was touching, and I didn't know how to handle it. I had to admit, it was nice having someone caring about me. But as nice as it felt, I was afraid the pain would be doubled when he decided he was done and began to ignore me. Not allowing my mind to go there, I dismissed the unpleasant thought as much as possible before nodding in reply, "Yeah...I'm sure." *Total lie.* "Come on, we need the truck. Follow me...Mom put it in my room."

I took off toward my bedroom with Barry trailing close behind. When reaching the doorway, I was about to enter when noticing he had come to an abrupt stop. As I turned, Barry stood there slightly pale-faced. Expressionless. Confused to what brought this sudden distress, I asked, "What's wrong?"

"Um...Nothing." As he eyeballed the room, his eyes were the only body part moving. I studied him while he remained standing still, unwilling to budge. Afraid of speaking, I remained quiet in fear of interrupting whatever he needed to process. After what seemed like forever, he released the breath he was holding. I was surprised he didn't pass out since much time had passed. "I'm sorry, it's..., It's just odd being in this house after all this time, I guess. Old memories keep flashing back. The last thing I want to do is scare you, but..." He hesitated before blurting out, "You're sleeping in Johnny's bedroom."

"My nightmares," I whispered. "Of course. This room is why he keeps visiting my dreams." It didn't occur to me that we had shared the same bedroom. In fact, I didn't even think about the possibility of where he had slept. *Wow.* That's the missing connection.

"Wait…What nightmares?" Barry asked, interrupting my revelation.

His stare penetrated through me as our eyes connected. The guilt from not telling him began to overshadow any excitement when his brows furrowed together in concern. "I haven't mentioned them, have I?"

In slow motion, he dragged his head back and forth without uttering a word. The tightness of his jaw was enough to show his anger, but the reasoning behind it confused me. *Was he upset about my dreams being invaded or my refusal of telling him?* Maybe it was a combination of both. I chastised myself for revealing my secret. But finding the link between the nightmares and Johnny was significant. It was yet another important piece to my imaginary puzzle.

Barry, still staring, waited for an explanation. Out of nervousness, I chewed on my bottom lip before admitting, "Every night since that first vision, I've had a reoccurring dream. That was until last night. I think he's trying to tell me something, but I always wake up before he says it. My last dream was different, though. I clearly heard the word *woods* before awaking."

Barry's jaw loosened as his brows smoothed out. The coloring in his face washed out again, leaving behind paleness. Instead of being angry, he seemed dismayed. I let out a small humorless laugh. "Now, who's scaring who?"

"No. You're not. I mean…I'm fine." He stumbled on his words, putting on a brave front trying in vain to hide his fear. "You amaze me. I don't know how you can stand here and act as if nothing bothers you. If it was me, I'd totally be freaked out."

"It's not bravery, believe me. More like…survival," I replied. "I've been different my whole life, so I guess I learned to deal with the weirdness a long time ago."

The exhaustion was taking over, and before continuing our conversation, I needed to sit. Not knowing if he'd follow me or not, I went over to my bed and sat on the edge. To my surprise, he followed sitting beside me. His curiosity must have been piqued because he no longer appeared afraid. That was good because it was taking all my strength to disclose any part of my history. If there were any trace of the fear being of me, I would shut completely down. Not usually sharing personal information, especially secrets, I found myself in new territory.

With a slight tilt of his head, his consuming stare stirred something deep inside me, and it took all my willpower to stop myself from reaching out to touch him. He confused me, but he also made me feel safe, which confused me even more. I blinked, trying to focus before continuing, "When I was little, I'd be playing with my friends. When one of them would touch my hand or arm, I'd visualize them in their home setting. It would be an argument they had with their parents the night before, or a happy occasion like playing in the park. Whatever strong emotion stirred inside of them was what I would see. Of course back then, I didn't worry about it. I thought it was normal until I entered junior high.

"I never mentioned being able to see segments of their life, partly because nobody had ever shared what they viewed, I thought it was a secret, like something that's supposed to be private. I remained quiet about them until a vision revealed one of my friends getting abused by her father. After telling my mother about it...Let's just say she didn't handle it well. At first, she didn't want to believe me. When the abuse became public knowledge, she sat me down and had me explain exactly what I had seen. Of course, doing what Mother does best, she decided to keep quiet about it, and told me never to mention what I could do to anyone."

I broke eye contact focusing on my balled fist in my lap when self-consciousness started creeping in. I just couldn't fathom the idea of him watching my face; I was so embarrassed to be displaying my life story.

In a tone barely over whisper, I continued, "That's when I started to withdraw from people. I didn't want to have these visions anymore and quit inviting friends over to avoid them. I made up excuses as to why I couldn't go over to their houses until they eventually quit asking."

I paused, wondering if I should admit this next part. Barry sat there patiently as I contemplated what to do. Never having trusted anyone to this extent before, I swallowed as I pressed forward. "I had a few friends that I talked to, but I didn't consider them close. I kept everyone at a safe distance because I didn't want to chance them finding out about my abilities. Mom made it seem like a curse, and I guess I did, too. I walked in the hallways of school, drifting along as an outcast among a sea of normal people.

"Everything seemed to be going okay. It wasn't great, but it was decent enough. That was until April went missing, and her sweater touched me. The vision was too powerful and frightening for me to hide my expression. And, well...you know the rest."

Still staring at my now white-knuckled hands, tears had begun to form. I tried to blink them away because the last thing I'd wanted to do was break down and cry in front of him. *God, when did I become such a sap?*

"Heather..." He came over, wrapping his arms around me, drawing me close to him. "Heather, I'm sorry you had to go through that. I'm here for you now if you want me to be."

My heart started beating faster as I stared back at him. We were close, sitting here on my bed with his arms wrapped around me. It just felt right. Perhaps if we had known each other longer, or I knew if he liked me for more than friendship, we would have shared a kiss. My body wanted to lean forward and let it happen naturally, but now wasn't the time. Instead, I backed away from him as his hands slid down to my waist. His fingers skimmed along the curve of my hips, sending sensations through me. My thoughts jumbled together, making it difficult to concentrate. His stare was captivating and if I knew how to read him, I'd swear he wanted to return that kiss. But that was impossible, nobody wanted me. The heat rising in my cheeks, as I realized how ridiculous I was being, broke the moment. "Thanks, Barry. You're a good friend to have." Placing my hand on his chest, I raised up, pretending not to notice how his head dropped in what appeared to be disappointment. Before I could read too much into it, I quickly added, "We better get started."

Barry quietly went over to my dresser picking up the truck as I took off toward the living room. If he was upset with me, he didn't show it. Instead he followed me out as if nothing had happened. Maybe I had read too much into it because he wasn't acting disappointed. *What do I know about guys' thoughts and feelings anyway—nothing, that's what.*

I went straight to the couch and sat down while never taking my eyes off the toy. This was really happening. I was voluntarily trying to have a vision while he sat right beside me. That thought made my stomach want to retch, as a choking sensation began deep in my throat. Barry must have sensed my anxiety because he asked me again if I was up to it. With the words "No, let's forget the whole mess" on the tip of my tongue, I whispered "yes" instead.

I closed my eyes trying my best to clear my mind as he handed me the toy truck. No surprise, Johnny immediately flashed in front of me. *He was in the backyard with his blue toy truck, the one I'm holding now. As a man approached him, he wasn't scared. He eyed the guy for a second and went back to playing. He had seen that man before, perhaps knew him. "Come here Johnny, I need to show you something," the guy said in a deep, husky voice. Johnny glanced at the guy then momentarily looked over to the house next door. "Come on, there isn't much time," the guy urged. Johnny glanced back at him before getting up to follow him into the woods, abandoning his toy.*

My body jerked as I flashed to Johnny sitting all alone in a room, unable to move. I could sense his body aching when he realized his arms and legs were tied up. Breathe...I could hardly breathe. Something seemed to be restricting my air flow. I realized a gag had been placed in his mouth as he struggled to work it loose.

A strong volt of energy zapped straight through my heart, causing my pulse to spike. Panic set in. As he desperately scanned the room, four dingy plain walls were all that he visualized. They clearly offered no sign of escape. There wasn't one distinguishing feature to the room, except the single doorway. Coldness overcame my body as I realized it must be a basement. Johnny, having worked his gag loose, began to cry. Through the sobs I could barely make out the words "I want my mommy."

Johnny's head snapped toward the creaking sound of a door opening slowly. My vision started to cloud making it impossible to see the guy coming toward him. He's there. I could sense his presence, but I couldn't see him clearly. My heart sank, knowing Johnny's tears were clouding my vision. Something flashed, catching my eye. It took a second to figure out it's a reflection from something shiny in his hand. My throat swelled shut. I needed to breathe, but I couldn't. He stepped closer. As his hands rose, I realized the shine reflected off a…

I inhaled sharply, gasping for air, as I snapped back to the present.

"Heather…Heather…It's all right. Look at me." A frantic voice shouted out.

I turned toward the voice calling my name, but it took a minute to focus as the fear slowly subsided. Too afraid to speak, I waited for my heart rate to slow while I tried evening out my breathing.

"Are you okay?" Barry asked apprehensively. His eyes were filled with nothing but concern as he gazed deeply into mine.

I wasn't sure why, but I hated seeing the worried expression on his face. It wasn't right. He shouldn't be burdened with my troubles. He shouldn't even be a part of this. He should be doing what most seventeen-year-old boys do and smiling his special smile that makes me pause. That was what I wanted for him, but if I was honest, I really wanted him not to be afraid of me. Slowly, I nodded my head. "Just give me a second," I said weakly.

He sat patiently next to me with his hand on the small of my back, waiting for my breathing to return to normal. When I found my voice, I screeched, "Barry, he knew his killer. It wasn't a stranger it was some guy who…" I remembered Johnny eyeing the house next door. I wondered if that was where the killer lived. It wouldn't be right to accuse anyone without more to go on, but it still made me wonder. "Who he recognized. He was playing in the backyard, with this toy, when the guy approached him and lured him into the woods."

"He killed him in the woods? You think he's buried there?"

"Maybe, but he didn't kill him out there. He bound him up to a chair and held him in a room without any windows. It was cold, like a basement. The walls were dingy. That's where…" I paused because the strained expression upon Barry's face told me he couldn't process any more information.

I had forgotten that he had been close to Johnny and realized I had thrown out too many random details. I needed to rein it in. Not thinking about the impact my words would have toward his feelings, I silently cursed myself for being too insensitive.

"I'm sorry. I don't have to continue if you'd like me to stop," I apologized.

Squeezing his eyes shut, he said, "No...go on. It's painful to hear, but it's the only way to find what happened to him."

With a slight hesitation, I decided to leave out the gorier details. I'd let those images haunt me instead. "The guy killed him in that room. I believe the room was in the basement of the killer's house. I also believe the house isn't too far away, that it's accessible by these woods."

Glancing out my window, toward the house next door, I wondered if I should say something. Honestly, I didn't know if he was killed in that particular house, but I couldn't shake off the sensation that it was somehow involved.

"You think the killer lives on this street?"

"Yes."

"Do you know which house?"

I answered cautiously. "Not exactly." I needed to make a decision quickly—tell him or not. If I kept quiet, and it turned out that was the place, then I'd never forgive myself. If I did tell him and that house had no specific role in his disappearance, then really what harm becomes of it anyway? Hard feelings from my next door neighbor I never talk to? I could handle that. I decided to tread the waters gently. "I have a suspicion, but I don't know for sure. When Johnny's killer lured him away, he did something. Which I hate to say since it's based on an assumption."

"What did he do?"

"The moment he recognized his killer, he glanced over at the house next door. I have a feeling it meant something, but that's all I have...a feeling. By not seeing him enter that house, I don't have any real proof. The one thing I have to go by was the murderer has dark hair with brown eyes, which I learned from my first vision. The guy I see coming out of that house," I pointed over to my neighbor's house. "Has grayish hair now. Was he living there ten years ago?"

"Mr. Barton?" Barry asked, wrinkling his nose in confusion. As he paused, I sat there quietly waiting for him to process the information.

"I wouldn't have suspected him. I always thought he was a bit odd, but not a cold-blooded killer. He was relatively new to the area when it happened, but he helped with the search party when they went out searching for Johnny in the woods. He came up to me one afternoon and told me not to be afraid; they would probably find him soon. Surely he wouldn't be behind it."

Pain, mixed with shock, dispersed across Barry's face making it difficult to process. I hated accusing that Barton guy of a heinous crime, but I just couldn't shake off the skepticism coming from that house.

With an attempt to ease Barry's mind somewhat, I offered, "Maybe he isn't behind it. Like I said, I have nothing solid." My eyes narrowed as I glared at his house, adding, "I just wish there was some way of getting inside there."

8 Betrayal

"I'm glad we have a chance to talk," Barry's friend, Nicole, said as we sat down at the cafeteria table. Our class ended a few minutes early which meant we had time before everyone else showed up for lunch. I had already gone through the lunch line, while she staked out our usual spot. With an eyebrow raised, I held my breath as she continued, "It's important to go to the police."

The surrounding acoustic level dropped about thirty decibels as the blood drained from my body in hesitation of her next words.

"Because they could help find what happened to Johnny," she continued with a hushed undertone.

The word *Johnny* whispered out of her mouth confirmed my fear and betrayal. It felt like a dagger thrust into my back. Shocked beyond words, I didn't know whether to be angry or hurt. *How could he do this to me? What was he thinking? What was I?* I knew better than to trust anyone other than myself. What a fool I was for putting my faith in him only to have it thrown in my face. A complete fool. I just got used to the idea of having somebody trustworthy in my life. Someone that was dependable, but now...I should have known better. In real life those people didn't exist. The balance between friendship and trust I craved was nothing but a pipe dream. Truth, reality bites. Everyone was self-centered and pushed along their self-agenda. Yeah, I was leaning more toward anger right now.

"Oh...Don't worry," Nicole quickly added, realizing by my expression that I was anything but pleased. As much as I tried remaining as stoic as possible, the anger must have shown because she suddenly became nervous. "I wasn't going to tell anyone because Barry warned you wouldn't want people knowing yet. What you can do is incredible, believe me, and I do hope you'll be able to find out what happened to Johnny. I just think you should get the police involved."

It took all of my willpower to sit there and listen to her ramble on about the police and Johnny. I wanted to get up and walk away, but in her defense, the fault wasn't hers. No...the fault belonged to Barry. I bit my bottom lip to prevent blurting out words that I might regret later and let her ramble. When I had enough, I replied very slow and very precise, "We can't involve the police until there's more to go on. Right now I don't have enough adequate information to contribute anything useful."

"But…"

"Besides," I rudely interrupted, not caring in the least what she was about to say. "It's hard convincing them about what I can do. First, they have to halfway believe in clairvoyance before they'll listen. It isn't easy."

"We can get them to listen. My uncle was lead detective on Johnny's case. He'll understand, I'm sure of it," she replied rather suddenly. My anger wavered at the enthusiasm embodying her voice. But then she lowered her gaze as her face fell. In a voice just above a whisper, she added, "Just promise me when the time is right, you'll go. I hope Johnny's disappearance can be solved, but what I really want is his murderer behind bars." Her eyes began to glisten making me wonder what her connection to him had been. Obviously she must have been close to him, which I guessed was the reason Barry told her.

With my anger subsiding towards Nicole, I softened my tone, replying, "I'd like that, too."

A gentle smile broke across her lips as she blinked away her tears. At that moment, Caleb joined us while dropping his tray down beside me.

"What's with you?" he asked, directing his question toward Nicole.

"Nothing…We're just having a heart-to-heart discussion. You know, *girl* stuff," she replied with a half-smile, composing herself rather quickly. As she straightened in her seat, she un-wrapped her sandwich as if we hadn't just had one of the most intense conversations of my life.

"Women." He shook his head as Barry and couple more friends piled in around us. "I'll never understand them."

When Barry smiled as he sat down across from me, I somehow managed a weak smile back, but I couldn't bring myself to meet his eyes. Still upset, I didn't want to be anywhere close to him. With my gaze dropping down to my lunch, I studied it as if it was the most intriguing macaroni and cheese I'd ever seen. Though my appetite disappeared, I didn't want to chance him noticing my expression. It would take him one minute to figure out how upset I was. Not wanting to risk him asking in front of everyone, I sat there toying with my food. I was miserable, knowing the bonds of trust between us were shattered, and I would never consider him trustworthy. It was a horrible resolution. I knew he'd hurt me one day, but I didn't expect it to be so soon.

As the group's discussion turned to last night's baseball game on television, I tuned everyone out. It was a habit to which I was accustomed, making it easy for me to fall back into my old tendencies.

What clouded my mind was the fact another person besides Barry knew about my abilities. It was pretty naive of me to believe nobody would find out. I mean, eventually it would come out. It's just…I wasn't ready for anyone to be aware yet. I certainly didn't expect Barry to go blab the first chance he got, either. I thought he understood my need for secrecy.

His betrayal upset me the most. Having somebody else know my secret was painful enough, but telling Nicole behind my back, that hurt. Not only was the knife plunged deep into my back, but as the seconds passed, he slowly twisted the handle, sinking it deeper. Sitting across from him was torturous.

All through lunch, the minutes ticked excruciatingly slow. I was pretty sure Barry kept glancing my way because the weight of his stare descended upon me heavily. I refused to give him any interaction as I blocked him, and everyone else, out. The need to escape was almost overwhelming. I wanted to run as far away as possible and be alone. At least when I was by myself, nobody could hurt me. Debating whether I should leave that instant or remain seated, I decided to stay. Leaving now would cause people to ask questions I didn't want to answer yet. So I sat there, feeling numb, while waiting for the bell to release me from my private hell.

After a grueling twenty minutes, lunch ended. I let out the breath I seemed to be holding as everyone started leaving. Nicole rose, and I noticed her slight hesitation before she made the correct choice and left. With no attempt to acknowledge her existence, I remained seated as she scurried off. But I wasn't alone. Barry didn't make an effort to move, either. As soon as everyone was out of hearing range, he leaned across the table and asked, "Are you mad at me?"

Extremely, I wanted to shout. Still not willing to glance his way, I stared at my uneaten lunch. As calmly as possible, I said, "I'm fine."

"Heather, don't play games with me. Something's bothering you, I can tell."

My eyes snapped up, boring directly into his as my voice came across icier than intended. "I have to get to class."

As I started to walk away, he raced to the end of the table grabbing my arm and said, "Heather... Wait."

I halted, turned my head toward him, and just glared. He dropped his hand quickly, as an understanding crossed his face before stating, "Nicole said something to you, didn't she?"

"How could you tell her?" I whispered.

"Heather, I..."

"Save it." I put my hands out to stop him from coming closer. "This is my fault. I should have known better." Pausing for a second, I shook my head then smirked. "I'm such an idiot. You know, I started believing you were different...that you understood where I came from. But it's a joke with me being the punch line. Well, I guess I was wrong about you after all. You're just like everyone else I've ever known—a huge disappointment."

As those words hung in the air, I turned and briskly walked away, trying to will away the image of his hurt stunned expression out of my head. It took all of my willpower to keep from running; I wanted to get away so bad. Without any detours, I headed straight toward my locker.

A little dazed, I stood in front of my locker, unable to open it. *What the hell's wrong with me?* I'd memorized the combination my first day here, but my fingers kept fumbling with the dial, messing it up. I needed to calm down. The background noise buzzed around me, replacing the normal banter that usually filled the hallways. When number thirty-five rolled into position, clicking the lock open, I gathered my belongings in a rush before heading to my car. Home was my only option because attending my afternoon classes wasn't happening. I was far too upset to even attempt to retain anything.

Upon reaching the car, I tossed my bag aside, slid behind the driver seat, and slammed my hands down on top of the steering wheel. With my eyes closed, I leaned my head backwards against the headrest and wondered why. *Why did he tell somebody, and why did he do it right when I finally started trusting him? Why couldn't he at least have warned me first?*

After a couple of minutes of sitting there, I tried to make sense of what just happened, but being that outraged, I couldn't think clearly. My mind was hazed over as if a thick fog filled my head where my brain once occupied. After a few minutes, when my mind became clearer, the anger faded. When I thought about how I treated Barry, I was embarrassed. After all he'd done for me, I couldn't believe I accused him of being like everyone else back in Clayton—or worse yet, calling him a disappointment. He didn't even come close to acting like them. Although he was wrong to tell Nicole about my ability, it wasn't fair of me to treat him that harshly. I guess being on my own for this long made me forget how to treat people. I don't know.

Disgusted and embarrassed with myself, I went home. The front curtain moved as I pulled into the driveway, reminding me that Mom was there. I totally forgot about her not working today. *How did I forget since I borrowed her car?* Shifting the gear into park, an audible groan escaped my mouth. Dealing with her was the last thing I wanted to endure. As I stepped out, I thought I'd better face her now and get it over.

"What are you doing home so early?" she asked as I walked through the door.

Before walking up to the house, I debated whether to make up an excuse, but I decided to tell the truth since she'd find out anyway. Besides, I wasn't in the mood to fabricate a story. After explaining to Mom about Barry, Nicole, and the way I handled it, the sympathy she expressed was more than I could bear. Although she drives me crazy, I hated being the reason behind her pain, and I kept doing it over and over.

"Sweetie," Mom stated as delicately as possible. "After all you've been through; I understand why you would be so guarded. It hasn't been easy for you, but ask yourself if you were fair to Barry." I groaned as she continued. "I agree, he shouldn't have told her without letting you know first, but, sweetie, he hasn't alienated you like every other person we've known. I'm sure he had his reasons. You need to at least listen to him, you owe him that much."

"I know you're right, Mom. Ugh! I probably blew any chance of having a real friendship," I yelled while throwing my hands up in the air.

"Don't be so hard on yourself. I have a feeling he'll be back around, so don't worry too much about it. Okay?"

"Thanks, Mom." I turned and headed toward my room.

Once nestled on top of my bed, I contemplated about what I was going to say to Barry the next time I saw him. Although part of me felt he should see things my way, I needed to apologize. I just wasn't quite sure how. As I closed my eyes, I feared tomorrow would come all too soon.

9 Appearances

The chimes of the doorbell rang throughout the house, pulling me from my slumber. Having had dozed off, it took a moment to wake up. After a few seconds I remembered coming home early because of an argument with Barry. Dread started to creep in as I wondered how badly I messed things up between us. When my eyes focused on the red digital numbers displayed on the alarm clock, I sat straight up as my brain registered the time. Not being able to contain the smile breaking across my face, I realized Barry must be here. School had let out twenty minutes ago, leaving no doubt in my mind who was here. Nobody else but Barry dared to visit.

Barry.

He's here. *Now?*

My heart began beating at a higher rate just from the idea of talking to him. I leapt out of bed, racing over to the dresser mirror. Displeased by my reflection, I grabbed my brush in a desperate attempt to tame the flyaway strands. Mom answered the door, which bought me a few extra minutes, but that was probably not good. It seemed to be causing further distress as reasons for his visit flitted through my head. *Did he come here to apologize, or say we're done? Or, worse yet, he wants to part ways after finishing what we started with Johnny.* My stomach became nauseous at the possibility of not being able to reconcile.

Mom came to my room, ending my internal conflict by announcing Barry's arrival. Regardless of his reasoning, I had to face him. A hair tie, lying to the side, made me abandon the idea of taming my frizzies. Without giving it any thought, I picked up the elastic band and placed my hair into a loose ponytail. With another glance in the mirror, I couldn't procrastinate any further. With a deep breath I thought, the sooner I faced the consequences of my behavior, the sooner I'd feel better.

As I walked toward the living room, Mom scurried off toward the kitchen to give us privacy. The idea of facing him had my stomach twisted in knots. As I rounded the corner, our eyes fell upon each other, stopping my forward motion. Speechless. Unable to move, he was tantalizing, standing there waiting for me.

That sudden urge to reach out and touch him came at me strong, but I didn't dare. There wasn't any way he would want me to touch him. The concern etched on his face caused a slight relief, forcing me out of my stupor.

"Hey," I whispered, barely finding my voice.

"Hey," he responded shakily.

The nervousness in his voice triggered my conscience. Even though I was embarrassed by the way I'd treated him, the tiny consolation from his lack of anger gave me hope.

"Let's go for a walk," I suggested, wanting nothing more than to be alone to talk privately. Mom wouldn't be hanging by the door listening, but I didn't want her quarantined to the kitchen either.

As we headed outside, we automatically turned and walked toward the woods. I wasn't sure what decided that course–the easier path would've been the sidewalk–but we gravitated toward it naturally. As we walked, it was clear, by the continuing silence, that neither one of us knew how to initiate the conversation. I should've been formulating a speech instead of falling asleep earlier. Now that he was beside me, that awkwardness hung above as we continued trekking deeper into the wooded area.

Much to my relief, Barry spoke first, breaking through the uncomfortable silence hovering overhead. "Heather, I need to apologize. I shouldn't have told Nicole without your permission which I realized too late. It's just...I got caught up in the possibility of finding out what happened to Johnny, I couldn't wait to share the news with her."

An unexpected twinge of jealousy zipped through me, wondering how close they'd been. Since I was a newcomer to town, their history was a mystery, and I mentally questioned whether they'd been a couple. *Was that why I got so upset?* She's beautiful, after all, it wouldn't be surprising. Long, blond hair with a perfect figure placed her in a higher, desirable playing field than me. *What if he still has lingering feelings?* As he continued talking, I forced myself to listen, dispelling any thoughts of them being together.

"My grandma used to babysit Nicole as well," he explained, answering my unspoken question. That information alleviated any turmoil brewing, allowing me to relax. "She played with Johnny more than me. The three of us were best friends, so she'd want to know, especially if there's a possibility of finding out what happened. Of course getting caught up in the excitement of telling her, I completely forgot about your feelings. The last thing I'd want to do is betray you. You have to believe that I'm truly sorry. Please forgive me, Heather."

The familiar log came within sight, and I wandered up to it, straddling the limb as I sat. Barry followed suit, sitting across from me. When my eyes grazed his face, he frowned as his gaze shifted downward. The remorse he displayed melted my heart, silently proving his actions weren't intentional.

There was no way I could've stayed mad at him even if I wanted to.

I lowered my voice replying, "I can understand wanting to tell her. I just wished you had given me a warning first. She surprised me, and I felt betrayed."

Noticing him wince at that word, I turned away before continuing. "Well, I owe you an apology, too. As upset as I was, I didn't mean what I told you. You've been so understanding and helpful from the beginning that I couldn't ask for a better friend."

"Thanks. I appreciate that. But you know..." He paused as the atmosphere turned serious. With a gentle touch, his hand moved part of my bangs to the left side of my face, drawing my eyes back at him. His stare penetrated deep into mine as he added, "I think about you as more than just a friend."

My breath hitched as it became hard for me to breathe, wondering if he was going to kiss me. My mouth went dry, making it hard to swallow. Never being kissed, I wasn't sure I was ready. Most people think nothing about the simple gesture, coming second nature to them without uncertainty. But in my case, it was taboo. Any form of personal touching had always been off limits as far as I was concerned. Nobody had been this close to me to cause worry, and I honestly wasn't sure what I wanted just now.

While I continued to stare back at him, my pulse quickened when he leaned closer. My thoughts became jumbled together, like one giant cluster ball of *what ifs*. He whispered softly, "I was hoping you felt the same way."

Still unable to utter words, our gazes locked. The seconds ticked by, but I didn't notice. Instead, they seemed to have halted as I'd lost sense of time. His sharp intake of breath made my eyes drop to his mouth as his lips parted. All my reasons to stay away vanished with the thought of those lips upon mine. The need to have him consume me was overwhelming. Incapable of fighting that urge any longer, our bodies collided, his soft lips pressed gently against mine. It was...magical. There weren't any visions or images racing through my mind. Just the yearning my body had for him.

After he pulled away, a tingling sensation continued as if my lips wanted more. I shuddered in response while Barry closed his eyes, taking in a breath. Upon opening them, his heated look made me blush. The corners of his mouth rose into his signature half-grin, but with an added dose of confidence. *God, he's handsome.*

"You know," he said as he grabbed hold of my hands, intertwining our fingers together. "We need to forget about this paranormal stuff for a while and go have some fun. I believe a real date is due. How about Saturday? Are you free?"

"Yes, of course." I continued blushing. He just asked me out on a date. Me. How my life came to this point, I'd never know. I was happy, and oddly enough, that was surreal.

"All right then, it's an official date."

He leaned in closer, kissing me one more time. I never would have guessed I could experience anything that great. It was wonderful. When our lips parted, I scooted toward him, resting my head on his shoulders. With his arms around me, I wanted to cherish that sense of contentment forever. Who knew how many moments like that I'd get to savor? As with everything else in my life, I should've known it wouldn't last.

The faint laughter of a little boy interrupted our tranquility, snapping my head sharply toward the right where the sound originated. "Did you hear that?" I asked apprehensively.

He gazed in the general direction I was staring, but shook his head no. "What exactly did you hear?"

"I'm not...sure. I guess nothing."

Unable to draw myself from staring over there, I was perplexed because a child had clearly laughed. *Why didn't Barry hear it?* Just as I questioned my sanity, I paled as an image of the boy from my visions came into sight. *Johnny?* With a quick glance at Barry, I couldn't believe he wasn't reacting. He stared toward the general vicinity of where Johnny's figure stood, but obviously wasn't visualizing the same thing as me.

I swallowed hard, composing myself before Barry could sense something was wrong. I closed my eyes, blinking them a couple of times, hoping to dislodge the image. Once I kept them open, Johnny remained standing there with much determination. *Is he trying to communicate to me?* His gaze bored into mine, causing me to shiver. He nodded, as if encouraging me, and raised his arm to point to something. Confused, I scanned the direction he pointed to, but nothing was there. When I examined it closer, a small clearing became visible.

The place wasn't far, approximately twenty yards away. The grounds, covered in old leaves with a few sporadic fern fronds, appeared to be about ten feet in diameter. I still didn't notice anything special, other than a cleared area. *What is he implying?* I turned toward Johnny's figure, mentally questioning him, but he offered no explanation. He kept cryptically pointing his finger toward that direction. *Does he want me to go over there?* As the thought fleeted, Johnny nodded as if in agreement before dissipating into thin air.

The current surroundings faded into the background as the clearing became the main focal point. I stepped off the log without a word and started walking to where Johnny guided me. He clearly was trying to show me something of importance, which I needed to find out what. *Why would you summon me over there Johnny?* The realization that something consequential was about to occur became stronger as I neared the area. Perhaps, revealing the most crucial piece to my imaginary puzzle.

"Heather, where are you going?" Barry's voice echoed through my clouded mind.

As if in a trance, I whispered, "over there," as I continued to press forward, picking up my pace. I needed to reach the place, now. I heard rustling sounds of movement and knew Barry was following. His quietness suggested he'd gotten used to my quirks, which was, in a sense, comforting.

Coldness crept through me as I reached the open space, causing me to shiver. My body swayed as lightheadedness came on strong. *I know what he wants. He wants me to find him.*

He's here…Somewhere.

But where?

With my arms spread outward, I closed my eyes, walking around the perimeter of the clearing. I could sense his presence. Although hard to explain, this suspicion penetrated deep inside of me, letting me know I was close. Advancing another six feet, I abruptly stopped, snapping my head toward the left.

I drifted over there skeptically, fearing what I was going to find. Deep down, I knew what lay below the surface. There wasn't any doubt in my mind, but this dreadfulness prevented me from speaking. I needed to tell Barry that Johnny sent me here for a reason. He wanted me to find him.

Determined to fulfill his wish, I continued. With only a few steps forward, tightness clamped in my chest, making breathing impossible. This tightness was unlike earlier, for this was a pain I'd never encountered. I dropped to my knees, clutching my arms against myself, while being mentally pulled in multiple directions. Hurt, mixed with a strong desire to start digging, overcame me. I remained still, fighting off this urge as I concentrated on breathing.

"He's here. This is where he's buried," I managed to gasp out.

I forced my head to turn away to focus on Barry instead. He stood there speechless with our gaze zeroed in on each other. The ashy coloring of his face betrayed his efforts of putting on a brave front. He was frightened. *Is this when he'll snap and run far from me as he can?* No matter how often he tried convincing me otherwise, I felt one of these days it'd be too much to handle.

"How...How do you know?" he squeaked out.

"It's hard to explain, but this sensation is overpowering... I just know." I wasn't about to tell him that Johnny's ghost pointed me in that direction. That was information I'd never share with anyone since they already thought I was crazy.

Barry stood there, staring at the spot. His contorted face revealed the raw, emotional pain he was enduring. I didn't have to be a mind reader to figure that out. But witnessing him going through that killed me. *When will I quit hurting him?*

"Johnny...," he muttered, breaking the silence. With tears swelling up, he fell to his knees, clutching both hands against his thighs.

With small steps, I walked over to him. As I approached him, I dropped to my knees, positioning myself in front of him. Two strong arms reached out, and pulled me into a firm, tight chest. Embraced in his arms, I never thought we would share a moment like that again, nor would I ever want to over these circumstances. But at the same time, I'd never felt that close to anyone in my entire life.

For once I was thankful for the capabilities bestowed upon me, since it brought us closer together. More importantly, it helped by finding his long, lost friend.

"Barry, it's time we go talk to Nicole's uncle."

After agreeing, we walked back home. Our hands were intertwined, but we remained quiet. The atmosphere was too heavy to engage in conversation. Besides, what's left to say after an encounter of that sort? When we approached the edge of the woods, Mr. Barton's house came into view. Not being able to shake the sensation that he was somehow involved, part of me wanted to go grab a hold of him to reveal his secrets. That'd be the quickest, easiest way. The possibility of him being a cold-blooded murderer prevented me from following through, but it was tempting nonetheless.

It would be nice to have solid proof that he was behind Johnny's death before going to the police. It would shed more credibility, forcing them to take me seriously. Some type of evidence was hiding inside that house. There had to be. Regardless, we needed to get in there. My mind wouldn't rest until we did.

10 Puzzles

Insomnia...the routine of late. Even so, tonight it was somewhat self-inflicted. As I lay in bed, I kept going over the events that occurred earlier today. The memories replayed over and over like a movie the cable channel constantly repeated. That did little to aid me into my nighttime slumber, but right now I wasn't sure I wanted to sleep anyway.

There was such a wide range of emotions that surfaced today; I believed I'd covered them all. The one overshadowing the rest was fear. I was afraid of closing my eyes, worried of what Johnny had in store for me tonight. Each night I dreamt about him, the dreams became more realistic. Like...I was having a one-way conversation with him. I'd come to the conclusion his way of communicating to me was through my subconscious state. That alone made me wary of falling asleep, especially after today. I think he only wanted me to help him, but what if I fail?

I'd never had any visions scare me before–they'd troubled me, but never scared me. Today that changed, because regardless of Johnny's intentions, I was shaken. I'd always accepted that I had talents above the norm, but seeing a ghost-like figure? Whatever that was delved deep into the supernatural. Unsure of my next step, or what could be done, I was completely lost.

Barry often looked at me with amazement at my resiliency regarding my visions, but I didn't know anymore. I was frightened. Not frightened from Johnny himself–he only wanted help–rather frightened over what the overall situation entailed. Previously, visions came at my will, but that particular situation was uncontrollable. What distresses me most was the possibility of where it may lead. *Am I opening up a gateway for spirits to contact me?* Since being clairvoyant was bad enough, possessing that type of ability was hard to fathom. Hopefully, I wouldn't be seeing any more *ghosts* in my future. That certainly wasn't my wish. The truth–I wished to be normal.

Once we convince the police to exhume Johnny's remains, maybe then he'd be at peace. My dreams could once again belong to me.

Before rolling over, I let out a small sigh. I was exhausted, and concentrating on Johnny wasn't helping, it was too daunting. I forced those thoughts away, shifting them toward Barry instead. It seemed to work–at least temporarily. The simple thought of him made a smile form while my hand rose unconsciously, touching my lips. The soft tenderness of his mouth pressed against mine made for incredible first kiss–one that I'd always cherish. But then, I started to imagine his arms wrapped around me. With my thoughts straying in this direction, warm sensations began flowing through me–heating places I didn't want to think about. This endearment was unexpected, and I wasn't sure how to handle it. But I did know, when he touched me earlier, the security that swelled inside me was amazing. *Who knew I'd enjoy having this level of affection from another person?*

As I continued to lie there, I tried with all my heart to reminisce about Barry, but even the sole vision of him couldn't keep Johnny away. The three of us were connected on too many levels.

The heaviness of my eyelids lured me into going to sleep, but I fought the urge to close them. Earlier, when we emerged from the woods, we sat on my back porch steps. We had remained quiet up to this point, each lost in our own thoughts. As we sat down, Barry broke the silence, asking, "When should we go see Detective Tanner…Now?"

"No, give me some time to think. I have to come up with a way to make him believe me. We can have Nicole call him tomorrow, I just…" Glancing over at my neighbor's home, I couldn't finish what I was going to say. I somehow got lost in the notion of that house being connected. I could sense it, but I wasn't sure how to prove it.

"Something's bothering you." He glanced over to where I was staring and frowned. "You're still wondering about Mr. Barton, aren't you?" he asked warily.

"Sorry, but I can't shake this feeling I have. We need to find out if any evidence exists inside his house before the police visit. When they come here I'm afraid he'll do something drastic."

"Good point. If he's guilty, he may try to leave once the police come, or hide some crucial piece of evidence."

"Then we'll never be positive if he's guilty." We sat there, defeated, as darkness started to descend upon us.

"We need to break in," Barry stated flatly, startling me with his devious ways.

Tilting my head to the side, I smirked. "Speaking from experience?"

"No." He chuckled. "But I do know where the janitor keeps his jimmy. I'll sneak it out so we'll have something to work with."

"His what?"

"His jimmy…a device to unlock doors. That's not its official name, but it's fitting since you jimmy the lock to…uh never mind. I've seen him use it multiple times on classroom doors. It should work for us. I've already seen his back door and we're in luck, it's a standard lock with no deadbolt."

Trying to hide my smile, I gazed at him with wonderment. Never having pegged him for a sneaking-around, criminal-minded person, I couldn't help but ask, "Just how do you plan on getting this device, or should I ask Mr. Deviant?"

He let out a laugh before answering, "I have my ways. When you're considered a *good* student you gain a lot of peoples' trust." With an arch of his eyebrow, he grinned mischievously.

We decided to break-in tomorrow afternoon after Mr. Barton left for work, or wherever he went at that time. That will leave us Thursday to talk to the detective. If they believe us, they can exhume his body by Saturday. Providing no mishaps occur, that was our plan anyway.

Not exactly sure what I expected to find, at least searching his house would put my mind at ease...

My eyelids kept getting heavier and heavier before I succumbed to the darkness of the night. Providing how badly my body needed this sleep, one would figure the last few remaining hours would be peaceful. Not in my case. Hardly any time passed before Johnny made his appearance inside my head. The dream started the same, with him playing in his backyard, but then changed. The tone suggested a sense of urgency. Flashes of previous visions kept popping up like a fast forward button was being pressed. Every scene came to an abrupt halt showing Johnny sitting by himself in a white room. In slow motion, he turned toward me with a tear-streaked face, and opened his mouth to speak. Next thing I heard was Johnny's voice saying the words "Christopher Warfelt."

To my dismay, I jolted out of the dream. I closed my eyes in vain, wanting desperately to fall back asleep. Please, if I could just sleep long enough, then I'd get to ask Johnny who Christopher Warfelt was. The adrenaline pumping through my veins wasn't going to allow any more sleep tonight, no matter how hard I pleaded. Finally conceding, I rubbed my face, and sighed. With great reluctance, I reached over to my nightstand and turned on my lamp. There wasn't any use fighting it. With a huff, I grabbed an envelope lying near the edge, and scribbled the name across it.

As I stared at what's written, I speculated who he could be. *Is he the killer?* Frustrated, I slammed the paper on the table, and flopped back down on the bed. This unsolved crime had yet another puzzle piece. Except that piece was oddly shaped with tabs that didn't fit into any of the other's. Still unable to sleep, I continued wondering if this mystery would ever be solved.

11 Trespassing

"**B**arry...Are you sure that's going to work?" I questioned as he was jamming the device in between the lock and doorframe. To me, it didn't appear that it would, much less in the timely fashion that we needed. As I stood beside him, I was getting anxious. I kept watch, paranoid that somebody would see us. We were relatively safe since none of the other neighbors were home yet. But that knowledge did little to calm my nerves.

"Sure, I just need to..." A clicking sound snapped through the air sending a thrill through my body. "See...? I knew what I was doing." He smirked, tossing his head confidently.

"Uh-huh." I laughed nervously, peering over my shoulder as Barry laid the device on the back step. We opened the door and entered with caution. As I took that first step into the house, I wondered why I talked him into this. It was probably a bad idea. *What if we get caught?* I wasn't sure what I expected to find, and it seemed like a huge risk to take for just pacifying my nerves. Not voicing any concerns out loud, I remained quiet. There wasn't any point in turning back now since we're already indoors.

The first room we stepped into was the kitchen. After a quick scan, my first thoughts led me to be impressed. He was a bachelor after all, and this room was immaculate. Nothing on the countertops was out of order. But upon deeper inspection, there appeared to be a reason behind the spotlessness–there weren't any items to be out of place. The only thing on the countertops was a set of stainless canisters which reminded me of the ones you'd find in a doctor's office. Instead of cotton balls, sugar would be the replacement. Just a teaspoon of sugar...

Astonished, I went over and opened a cabinet door, trying to dispel childhood melodies out of my head. As I pulled the door open, I was taken aback by the systematic order. Everything was in its place, organized, and labeled accordingly. Every can, by vegetable, color, and size, lined up. First the greens...tall can of asparagus, French cut green beans, peas then moved to the yellows...creamed corn, yellow corn, and the small shoe peg corn...It was creepy.

Barry came up beside me, glanced inside, and said, "This guy's wacked."

A small laugh escaped as I agreed. "Yeah, but let's go try to find something other than small greens."

The house was small, something for which I was thankful. Given our time constraint, it shouldn't take long to search everything. Basically there was a hallway dividing the house into two sections. From the west side, I'd previously noticed four windows, which I assumed were bedrooms and apparently his kitchen. The east side–the one facing my house–held the living room and probably the bathroom.

Earlier we had decided to start in the main room, make our way through the bedrooms, and then search the basement. As we turned to leave, Barry bowed as he extended his right arm saying, "Ladies first."

I smiled suggestively at him, loving his goofiness.

When I stepped through the doorway leading into the hallway, my smile dropped instantly as I came to an abrupt halt. My breath caught when a darkened aura descended upon me, encapsulating my body. I swallowed hard as the strangulating sensation tried taking over. Straight across from me was a single door, which had me mesmerized. Most people would just see an ordinary, solid-pine door. But there wasn't anything normal about that one, it was dark, sinister. As if holding me captive, I narrowed my eyes while continuing to glare. It wasn't hard to figure out where the door led. The negative vibe emitting from it left little doubt that it opened to the basement. I couldn't pull my eyes away as it continued to tantalize me.

An image of Johnny being dragged through the doorway flashed through my mind, and I wondered if he was conscious before being placed in that pit. The thought of him suffering through an experience like that made bile creep into my throat. That nauseated feeling kept me glued to my spot.

At some point, we had to go down there, but not now. Earlier, we both agreed to investigate that room last, and considering how I felt, that was a smart choice. Once I entered the same room where Johnny was placed, I knew my vision would be strong. Before that happened, we needed to find solid evidence against Mr. Barton. Proof would be needed for the police to have a chance at arresting him. My vision wouldn't hold up in court, and I wanted this guy convicted.

Barry, who seemed to understand my purpose for staring at that door, broke through my trance by gently nudging me. As I followed him to the living room, I kept peering back. The uneasiness wouldn't go away, but I needed to concentrate on our current task as we entered the main room.

It took a whole two seconds to realize that room was as orderly as the kitchen. After quickly scanning his house–the parts readily visible–that seemed to be the consistent theme. Very impersonal. There weren't any knickknacks or pictures displayed. If I didn't know differently, I'd say nobody lived there. This impersonal void of a home put me in mind of a staged house–an empty house for sale that had been planted with furniture, waiting for the next unsuspecting buyer. But this wasn't a staged home. No, someone lived here, but there wasn't any proof. It had a strong sense of sterility about it, a sharp coldness which made us afraid to touch anything in fear of contaminating it.

I fleetingly wondered if we should have removed our shoes–if any drop of dirt, or tracking of footprints showed, our cover would be blown—but checking behind us, we didn't appear to be leaving any trail. We lucked out because the carpet was older Berber, which didn't show footprints. After a brief inspection of the room, there wasn't anything significant. Moving on into his bedroom, we bypassed the *guest* bedroom. Barry went over to inspect it, but the room was completely empty. I guess there wasn't a need for furniture since he apparently never had guests. Strange, you'd think he'd at least have a desk.

"Look for a small box or something similar," I said, entering his bedroom. "Sometimes the killer will keep items from their victims as a souvenir, or something that will glorify them like a newspaper article. And make sure you place everything back the way you found it. He's very detail-orientated, and will know at once if someone's been in here."

Upon opening his closet, unsurprisingly his shirts and pants lined up perfectly. If the kitchen was any indicator, I half expected it. What did surprise me was the shirts and pants being the same color—tan and brown, respectively. *How boring is this guy's life?* A little flabbergasted, Barry came up beside me, peeking in.

"This guy has a serious compulsive disorder," he said shaking his head.

"Obsessive compulsive disorder isn't a crime, but this man seems strange. Hmm. Since you're taller, take the upper shelf, while I take the lower half," I directed.

After thoroughly searching through his closet, we didn't find anything. After checking underneath the bed, and all through the dresser drawers, we still came up short. Frustration set in rather quickly, and if I didn't clear my mind, I'd make a mistake. I turned, walking over to the back wall. With my back against it, I placed my hands to the side of my head as I slid down into a crouch position. Think...I need to think. What am I missing? He was involved, I could sense it, but I was overlooking something.

Unmistakably irritated by this point, I sat there knowing there wasn't any other choice but to go down to the basement. Evidence or not, I had to find out if he was Johnny's abductor. I dreaded that vision, but to be positively sure Mr. Barton's guilty, I had no other choice.

Actually, I was surprised by my lack of visions thus far. Being short on time, I'd been careful on what I touched, but I would've thought something would've happened by now. He must not be attached to anything in this house.

Of course it could be that Mr. Barton's innocent, and there was nothing for me to see. We may be breaking into his home for no reason—the thought had crossed my mind. I'd feel bad if that was the case, but I didn't believe he was innocent. There weren't any warm, cozy feelings inside that house. Nothing but evil. When I viewed that basement door, I swear it was present.

The thought brought shivers that forced me to take a deep breath. Upon opening my eyes, I stared straight ahead. The amount of light filtering in through the curtains had lessened, alerting us that nighttime was fast approaching. Then it hit me. There should be two windows in here. I'd been coming home enough times to know there were four of them along the west side—three long and one short. The front bedroom had one, and the smaller window was in the kitchen. *Where's the fourth?*

When I stood back up, another thing occurred to me, the room wasn't proportionate. The wall with the closet seemed too close. I jolted up and dashed toward the hallway. Barry, a little stunned, asked, "What's the matter?"

"Something's off with this room. The size is wrong, it's too small."

Following me out still confused, he asked, "Like what?"

"Look at the south side wall in proximity to the inner kitchen wall. Besides, we seem to be missing a window in here. The room is supposed to have two."

"You're right. They don't," he exclaimed. "Here's where the wall is and it's clearly not lined up with the kitchen." He ran down the hallway, pointing out where it should've been. From the kitchen wall, they were a good five feet apart.

Our eyes met as I whispered, "A secret room. But where's the entrance?"

We both hurried toward the kitchen. His hands moved quick, working them along the wall. "Nothing here. It has to be in the bedroom," he murmured.

With that we scurried back to the bedroom, anxiously wanting to find that opening. Once we stepped through the door, we glanced at the south wall. Together we said, "The closet."

He wasted no time in pounding along the inside walls of the closet. After hitting the side facing west, it vibrated. Excitement began racing through me as I watched him study the wall. After a few seconds, he muttered, "Ah."

With his hand placed on a concealed block of wood, the wall swung open after he gave it a tight pull. Intrigued, we walked through it carefully, trying not to knock over anything. We were close to finding out his secrets which made it hard not to rush. The one thing rushing, though, was my heart. It raced from anticipation, I was so excited.

As we entered, I quickly scanned the entire area. Small sized, painted in a boring off-white color, the walls were bare except for the missing, large window. If it wasn't for the tiny wooden desk and two-drawer matching file cabinet, the room would be empty. On top of the desk sat a lamp and a pad of paper with a pen adjacent to it. *Such order.*

Giving Barry a peek, he wore an expression I couldn't quite interpret, but made me sad. I couldn't imagine what went through his mind. Betrayal, perhaps, that dated back ten years. With the heartbreaking glance, he nodded as if in agreement with my thoughts. I replied with a tight smile before we began searching through Mr. Barton's belongings. Barry started with the file cabinet while I tackled the desk. Pressed for time, we worked quickly. The search shouldn't take long, since there was only two pieces of furniture, but we were close to getting the truth. Not knowing quite what to expect, I knew something had to be there.

We continued searching, hoping to find anything that would connect everything together. Our tension escalated at the absence of anything incriminating. I honestly thought with this room being secret, we would have found something by now, but most of the drawers were empty. That didn't make any sense to me. Barry wasn't having any luck either and had actually finished. He came over to stand by me while I had one last drawer to snoop through.

"Well, this is it," I said, taking in a deep breath as I opened the last drawer. Disappointment loomed over me again as the drawer revealed nothing but emptiness. Anger mounted quickly, at the thought of wasting a big portion of our time for nothing. In my frustration, I let out an "ugh," while slamming the drawer shut.

"Wait," Barry yelled out as soon as the drawer closed, echoing the slamming sound.

Startled, I asked, "What?" as he went to reopen it.

"Look, this drawer isn't as deep as the others," he said, pointing out the discrepancy. Upon closer inspection, the drawer did appear shorter. Barry made a fist and knocked it against the back of the drawer. The wood shifted. Whipping our heads toward each other, our eyes grew at the astonishment of our find. Collecting our thoughts, we quickly focused our attention back on the drawer. Barry hit it harder this time, and it shifted enough where he could move it out of the way.

With a gasp, I stared at the faux drawer in bewilderment. I couldn't believe what I saw. Inside the hidden compartment was a meager, cigar-style box.

"Barry, you found it," I exclaimed. Afraid to touch it, I stood there for a second, envisioning what could be inside. That was it, what we'd been searching for. Barry reached down swiping it up. He placed it carefully on the desk and inhaled deeply. His eyes drifted toward me for a second before lifting up the lid.

I held my breath before peeking in. Expecting to see something about Johnny, I was surprised to see a driver's license, passport, and social security card. I wanted to scream. Clearly disappointed, my eyes flashed to Barry with the intent to complain, but stopped short. With a solemn face, Barry was staring down at the forms of identification.

Thinking perhaps I missed something, I inspected the driver license closer. Then I noticed why Barry looked so serious. "Is that...Mr. Barton?" I asked, already knowing the answer. It was those eyes...The same eyes that haunted my visions.

"That's his picture, but that's not his name. What's going on here?"

"He must be planning on changing his name to...Samuel Bates." Our eyes drew towards each other for a second, and I knew we shared the same thought. *Why would he need to change his identity?*

Barry asked, "Do you know what this means?" I stared at him, too dumbfounded to speak, as he continued, "I think he's planning on escaping, and he's changing his identity when he leaves. Heather, innocent people don't have spare identities lying around." Raising his voice, he continued, "And they certainly don't have them hidden in secret compartments in a secret room."

Nodding, I reread the name one more time. "Barry, I think we should get down to the basement before it gets too late."

Agreeing, he placed everything back carefully and was closing the drawer when we heard the front door shut.

Our heads snapped toward the sound, then back toward each other. I mouthed *crap*, knowing full well that it was Mr. Barton coming home early. I didn't know what to do. We were stuck in this room with only one way out. *How on earth are we going to get out of here?* Barry placed his finger to his mouth, signaling for me to keep quiet as he crept over to the hidden doorway. Peeking out, he grabbed its side and closed it slightly, leaving only a sliver of an opening. Being sealed in here would be the last thing we wanted to happen.

Moving wasn't an option for me as I stood there paralyzed by fear. I didn't know what we were going to do. Barry looked back at me and must have seen the panic on my face because he mouthed, "It'll be okay."

Grabbing a hold of me, he backed us up against the wall. He must have been assertive enough because my body responded to his authority without hesitation. Seemingly convinced I was secure, he stood in a protective stance, guarding me. I wasn't sure what he was planning on doing if Mr. Barton came through the door because he didn't have any weapons on him aside from his fists. The only thing this room had to offer was the table lamp. Regardless, Barry was ready to pounce.

As Mr. Barton took off walking down the hallway, I tried slowing my rapid breathing. His footsteps sounded closer until they came to a stop, silencing the entire house. Barry's arm tightened against my chest, pressing me behind him. Standing there seemed like a lifetime when I finally heard his footsteps start again. That offered no comfort since the shuffling sound of his feet was getting louder. It didn't take a genius to figure out he was in his bedroom. A creaking sounded as the closet doors opened, vibrating through the walls, which placed him just a few feet away from us. I held my breath, trying to be as quiet as possible. It felt like my chest was going to explode, my heart was racing. I feared any minute he would decide to burst through the hidden door.

Barry stood there like a soldier, protecting me with his arm still pressed against me. I would have thought he'd be tired, holding that position for so long, but he stood there solidly. Shifting my eyes over toward the lamp, I was definitely going to grab a hold of it as soon as Mr. Barton came in here. Barry would, no doubt, lunge for him giving me ample enough time to grab it.

Being able to tell the two apart may be a problem since darkness had definitely settled in. The light from the outside streetlamps shone through the window, but didn't offer much help. It danced around the room, emitting shadows and further heightening our awareness of the danger we were in.

The sound of the closet door closing made me relax a bit, and I slowly let out the air I was holding as his footsteps started to rescind. But then silence prevailed. My breath hitched as the noise shifted toward escalating footsteps. He was heading back toward the closet. Barry positioned himself a little more in front of me as I noticed his hands balled up into fists. This is it, I thought.

Any second, he'd come in here and find us. Eyeing the lamp, I mentally pictured myself grabbing a hold of it and smashing it over his head.

As the footsteps sounded a few feet away, I swallowed hard. He stopped, pausing for a minute. I wondered what he could be doing. *Did he realize we're in here and he's toying with us?* The closet door opened again, rippling fear through my entire body. I took a deep breath and held it. Holding as still as I could, I mentally prepared myself to lunge for the lamp. He went to the secret door and opened it slightly. Then for some reason, he slammed it shut trapping us in here for however long. As we heard his footsteps leading out of the bedroom, I let out my breath in relief. Shifting slightly, for my body started to cramp from being still too long, I felt somewhat relieved.

Barry moved his arm down, away from me. "We'll have to escape through the window," he whispered.

Turning toward the window, I didn't think that was a doable option. But since we certainly couldn't leave the way we came, our choices were pretty limited. Straining to hear where Mr. Barton was headed to, it sounded as if the bathroom door opened.

As the slamming of the door vibrated through the air, Barry whispered, "Now."

Surprisingly my body responded by taking off toward the window, without saying a single word. Barry rushed over there carefully moving the curtains away. He quickly unlatched the lock and tried pulling up on the window. Of course it barely budged. As feared, it was sealed shut. Those older-style windows, that had been painted multiple times, never wanted to comply. Immediately, he pulled out a pocket knife and began cutting through the layered paint. With another hard push, it finally raised. Relief washed over me as I let out a breath. He didn't mess around with the screen, immediately kicking it out of our way.

Climbing out, I eyed the ground, which caused me to hesitate before jumping. It really wasn't that far down, but it made me nervous nonetheless. Sucking in a huge breath, I jumped off the ledge, landing on the ground with a big thud. Pain jolted through the right side of my body, but I was elated to be free from that room. Barry jumped next, a little more gracefully than me.

As he caught up to me, I started off toward the direction of my house, but staggered backward when Barry grabbed a hold of my arm. Flipping me around, he pushed me toward the direction of the woods. We ran until we got to the edge and Barry yelled, "Wait."

Stopping, I turned toward him and said, "We need to go farther."

"I have to go back and get that tool. I need to return it to school tomorrow, and it's still on the step."

With a glance at Mr. Barton's house, my heart sank at the sight of it lying there on the bottom step. I had forgotten all about it and knew we couldn't just leave it. My eyes flashed to the backdoor and a slight relief spread through me. Thank goodness, we had enough common sense to shut it.

A whole new batch of worry spread throughout my body as Barry said, "Stay hidden while I go get it."

Before I could protest, Barry took off, sneaking back up to the Barton house. He stayed low to the ground as I stared wide-eyed at the kitchen windows. Barry snaked his way up there and just as he started to grab the tool, the kitchen lights flicked on. Barry snatched it up, dropped to the ground, and scurried toward the side of the house.

My breath caught, bringing my arm up to my chest. Placing my hand over my core, I thought my poor heart would never be the same. Quickly ducking behind a large white oak, I stood there, panting for a second. I sneaked my head around the tree trunk to get a glimpse of what was happening. Barry was still lying low against the ground, but right when I gazed back toward the window, Mr. Barton's face popped in it. Sucking in a breath, I ducked behind the tree, praying to God he didn't notice me.

It seemed to take forever, but the light finally clicked off, allowing Barry to hurry his way back over to me. Without missing a beat, we took off running through the woods, not slowing down for anything. The briars were snagging at my clothes and skin, and I kept tripping over roots, but I didn't care. We just kept running.

Once out of sight from the backdrop of the houses, we finally came to a halt. Panting, I was trying to catch my breath as I whispered, "Oh my God, Barry. What was he doing home this soon? He almost caught us."

"I know," he said, equally out of breath. "I had us come in here because I was afraid he'd see us cut across the lawn and didn't want him knowing it was us. He'll know someone's been in there, though, since the back door is still unlocked, not to mention what I did to the screen. He's too neurotic not to notice."

"Yeah…You're right. What should we do?"

"Nothing…He can't prove it's us, and I don't think he'll want the police involved anyway." With one last scan of the area, he placed his hand upon my back as he said, "Let's get you home."

With the darkness of the night upon us, it was difficult walking through the woods. A scant amount of moonlight filtered in through the tree branches, dancing along the ground, but everything seemed black regardless. We had a flashlight with us, which would have made it much easier, but we were afraid of being seen if we turned it on.

He held onto my hand as we slowly maneuvered ourselves through the woods. I couldn't believe we ran this deep. Not exactly sure which way was out, I let him lead the way. The howling of nearby coyotes startled my already frayed nerves causing me to inch closer toward him. As the gap between us closed, his arm wrapped protectively around me. We edged our way through the brush, but being joined together made it more difficult. I didn't care because I felt safer with his arms around me. Finally with his Grandmother's house in sight, we walked out of the woods toward her back porch. We sat there for a second, letting our nerves calm down.

"We definitely need to see that detective tomorrow, in case Mr. Barton is planning on leaving. I mean, he has false identification for some reason." I spoke, breaking through the silence. I think we were both too frazzled to speak at first and were sitting there waiting for something. I just wasn't sure what that something was.

"I was thinking the same thing. But don't you think we should have Nicole call him tonight?"

I hesitated before answering. Much to my disappointment, we didn't prove that Mr. Barton was connected with Johnny's disappearance. Finding false identification didn't make him a killer, no matter how odd it seemed. But there wasn't any doubt in my mind he was involved, I'd recognize those eyes anywhere.

I knew if we told the detective about my presumption, he couldn't do anything about it without some type of proof. We needed to get into his basement, but I was afraid if we tried again tomorrow night, it might be too late. Besides, he'd be more alert now once he realized somebody had been in his house.

"Heather?" Barry prodded.

"Um, Can we wait until tomorrow?" I pleaded.

His eyebrows drew together, no doubt questioning my sanity. "Yeah, I guess so, but I think it'd be better to call now."

I bit my lower lip, contemplating what to do. Once the call was made, there'd be no going back. My secret would be revealed, but how was that fair to Johnny? It wasn't, and I was being selfish. "You're right. We should have Nicole make the call, tonight."

"Are you sure?" he asked, reaching for his cell phone. With a nod, I sucked in my breath as he dialed her number.

I sat beside Barry as he started to explain to Nicole. An audible gasp sounded through the phone when he revealed where Johnny was buried. I closed my eyes, wishing I could stop her pain, but nothing was going to erase ten years of grief.

Barry pressed end and faced me. "She's calling her uncle now," he explained.

After what seemed like forever, she called back, confirming a meeting with the detective. She set it up after school tomorrow since he wouldn't be back in town until that afternoon. With assurances to her uncle that she wasn't in immediate danger, he agreed, but that meant we'd have to wait the entire school day. It was going to be a very long day.

"You think it's safe to go back home yet?" I asked hopefully. There was homework looming over my head, but I didn't think I would be able to concentrate. I was so exhausted.

"Yeah, I need to be getting home anyway." Barry sighed. "Let's go say good-bye to Grandma, and then I'll walk you over to your house. We'll go through the front door. I think if we act normal, he won't be as suspicious." With a shrug, he added, "I'm afraid if we act like we're sneaking back, our cover will definitely be blown."

"Good idea."

Trying to compose my face to reflect one of certainty, we went inside and told his grandma good-bye. She was such a nice lady and didn't even question where we had been. I wasn't sure if she could sense our apprehension, but she certainly didn't seem to suspect anything.

After talking briefly to her, Barry walked me over to my front door as promised. I noticed the curtain moving on Mr. Barton's window and what little confidence I had suddenly drained from my body as my hands started to shake.

"Barry, he's watching us through his window," I whispered under my breath.

Peering directly at me, he said, "I know. Calm down, he can presume. There's no proof and like I said, I'm sure he doesn't want the police coming over." Leaning closer to me as he was talking, he reached down and placed his lips on mine.

Forgetting about everything else, I simply enjoyed the moment. His lips felt so warm and tender against mine that all I wanted to do was stay there and kiss him all night. As the kiss became deeper, my hands found their way to his head. His hair was soft as I ran my fingers through it, which elicited a small moan from him. Pulling me closer, feelings ignited deep inside as my body seemed to crave more. I gasped, which caused the kiss to become aggressive. His tongue slid across my teeth, causing me to open my mouth to invite him in. Our tongues danced with each other as his hands wandered all over my body. They caressed my neck, trailing a path down my back where they eventually landed on my hips. Everywhere his hands touched left a tingling sensation, and my body seemed to be greedy, wanting more.

Panting, I had to break away. Staring at each other for a few seconds, neither one of us said a word as we both tried to catch our breath. When my breathing finally began to even out, I reluctantly whispered, "I need to get inside."

Lowering his head onto mine, he sighed. "Fine...I'll see you tomorrow at school then." He kissed me on top of my forehead, running his fingers along the side of my face. With the smile I love, he leaned over and kissed me quickly one last time before taking off. Once I got inside, I knew I had a long night ahead of me, followed by an even longer day.

12 Signs

Completely exhausted before crashing, I figured my sleep would be dreamless. At least that's what I'd hoped, but it ended up being wishful thinking. Johnny invaded my mind yet again. But this dream had a different sentiment. When he faced me, there weren't any streaming tears. Instead, the corners of his mouth turned upward as if trying to smile before whispering, "*So close.*"

With a catch of my breath, I woke up abruptly. I glanced at the alarm clock and wanted to scream as the red lights flashed four-fifteen. Three hours and fifteen minutes wasn't enough time to get me through the day, but it was useless to try going back to sleep

Of course being sleep-deprived didn't help any the next day at school. By fourth hour, as I struggled with consciousness, I realized I should have stayed home. After finishing some of the homework assignments, I dozed off around one in the morning. It was no wonder I was tired today.

In class, as I sat fighting to stay awake, I wished I had at least tried to sleep. It was pointless being here since I wasn't even listening to Mr. Wilson. His flat, monotone voice did little to hold my attention as my mind kept reverting to last night's dream...

After the shock abated, my brain registered the fact I wasn't frightened anymore. Johnny's hopeful expression, when he mentioned being close, was more astonishing than scary. He was encouraging us to continue. That was how I interpreted it, anyway.

While trying to shield a yawn, my eyes closed for a second as I pondered what Johnny said. I knew we were *close* to finding his body, that was a given, but did he mean something else–like figuring out his murderer?

I tried not to get aggravated, but it was hard. He could give better clues to work with, rather than these cryptic signs. Understanding why he only speaks a couple of words at a time, instead of complete sentences, would also be nice. Trying to stifle another yawn, my eyes grew heavier as I figured that question had no answer...

"Miss Reiner, would you like to repeat the last sentence I spoke?"

My chair jarred underneath me as Nicole kicked the legs from behind. The vibrations shook me out of my slumber as my eyes opened to the scrutinizing stare of my teacher, Mr. Wilson, hovering over me. Quickly realizing I had dozed off in class, I heard people laughing as I straightened up in my seat. Although slightly embarrassed, I also felt a sense of relief since I didn't have a glob of spit hanging from my mouth.

"Um…Sorry, sir, I didn't get much sleep last night," I replied, hearing more jeers around the classroom.

Mr. Wilson's eyes swept across the room, silencing everyone with his penetrating glare. Turning back toward me, he simply stated, "Make sure it doesn't happen again, or you'll be spending your time in detention with plenty of time to mull it over."

"Yes, sir."

As he turned around to walk back to the front, I shot Nicole a look of appreciation. She nodded back at me, but wore a concerned expression upon her face. Turning my attention back toward the front of the room, I was thankful for her warning. If it hadn't been for her, I probably would have slept through his scorning and ended up in detention. That certainly would have delayed us going to the police station, and I didn't need any more delays.

What I needed was to get the case solved so I can get some sleep.

After the bell rang, Nicole rushed up to me, asking if I felt okay. As we took off toward the cafeteria, I started to explain how we broke into Mr. Barton's house yesterday, but stopped. I wondered if Barry would want me telling. She started to ask something about Johnny, but we were interrupted when Barry and Caleb started walking up to us.

As Barry and Caleb approached, I knew Nicole desperately wanted to talk, but she hid her anticipation well. While Caleb finished his story, Barry shot us an apologetic look. We stood there patiently waiting until Caleb finally quit talking. Poor guy had no clue none of us wanted to listen to him. He didn't seem to notice, though. As he left to stand in the food line, Nicole demanded, "All right guys, spill. How do you know where Johnny's buried?"

"Well," Barry replied in a hushed voice. "Heather discovered where, but I can't really explain it." Glancing at me for backup, I gave him a wary smile.

"It's hard to explain, but I know. I could sense it. Did your uncle seem receptive to the idea?"

"Well, I told him that I needed to talk to him. That *we* needed to talk to him, but I didn't elaborate."

Caleb, along with the rest of the crew, had rejoined our table, promptly shutting down any further discussion about Johnny. While they joked and discussed such trivial issues, I thought how nice it would be to live without being constantly bothered by things. To not live a life surrounded by other people's despair and worry. I couldn't even imagine how that felt.

I tried not to dwell in my own self-pity because that wasn't going to change anything or make anything better. I just had to cope with what nature gave me and go forward with it. I would drive myself insane if I tried to figure out why I, of all people, was given such unique talents.

I think Barry was right in saying I needed to channel it for the greater good. If I could turn my negative to a positive, then I'd be able to cope with it better and perhaps live the rest of my life in some type of peace. While observing their friends and listening to their voices, I was going to start living in the now, as Barry puts it, and put an end to these internal battles.

Just as I started to feel confident, Nicole's cell went off. As she drew her eyes together, she mumbled, "It's my uncle." As she left to answer it, my heart skipped at the possibility of the appointment being cancelled. Something may have occurred to cause a delay. Barry shot me a sideway's glance, but other than the quick reassurance nod, he acted like everything was normal.

"What's this I hear about you falling asleep in Mr. Wilson's class," Caleb asked, pulling me from my mental meltdown.

Suddenly blushing, I had to smile. As embarrassing as it was, I wondered if the entire school knew by now. Barry smirked at me as I explained, "I didn't get much sleep last night. I stayed up late working on homework."

"You're lucky he didn't give you detention. He usually does, which means he must like you or something," he continued with his teasing.

Quickly realizing that I wanted the attention off of me, Barry interrupted, asking Caleb a question about the upcoming weekend. Grateful for the escape, I slipped back into my comfort zone of playing the listener.

The anxiety churned in my stomach when Nicole returned to the table. The casual way she flipped her hair concealed her own apprehension. I wasn't sure how she did it, but the way she disguised her emotions was skillful. She should go into acting. When she shot us a quick smile, my body relaxed knowing the meeting was still a go.

I breezed through the rest of the lunch period. My focus improved, either from the food I'd eaten, or knowing that we'd overcome the first obstacle. Whatever the reason, it was refreshing to have my second wind. Funny, how positivity could affect your alertness.

When lunch ended, Nicole waited for the rest of the gang to leave before speaking. She confirmed our meeting, explaining the call was him verifying the time. At least we were still meeting him right after school. Barry's driving us there, which will take a few minutes longer than I anticipated since his office was in the next town over. My adrenaline started racing again as the realization sunk in that we were getting toward the end. In a way, I could sense Johnny's own excitement. I was sure that was my own imagination, but the puzzle pieces were finally fitting together creating a disheartening, but beautiful picture.

13 Interrogation

"Can I help you?" The monotone voice of the receptionist rang through the semi-deserted room. The place was vacant except for one couple off to the left. They had this don't-mess-with-me attitude, acting like they'd punch the first person who'd dared to cross them. Tattoos sleeved his arms while studs and spikes lined her lips and eyelids. But that wasn't the intimidating part, it was their hostile expression. I tried not to stare.

"We're here to see Detective Steve Tanner," Nicole stated. Her voice was filled with such confidence; I was impressed. She sounded as if coming here was an everyday norm for her.

"Just one minute, I'll let him know you're here," the receptionist said with a hint of a smile.

As the lady picked up the phone, I was overcome by exhaustion. Apparently, my lack of sleep had caught up with me again. I needed to sit, and quick. After panning around the room, I stumbled over to some chairs in the corner, far away from the hostile couple. My second wind had completely drained away, leaving me worn out.

When I sat down, a sense of déjà vu occurred. I shivered at the remembrance of the stale-colored, block walls. That scene was far too familiar as it brought back the painful memories of talking to the detective back home. Closing my eyes, I took a deep breath, mentally praying I wouldn't have to fight as hard to convince Nicole's uncle about my abilities.

Back home, it was disastrous trying to get them to listen to me. The detective mocked me the entire time I tried explaining what I had envisioned. Finally, I had enough. Throwing my hands up in the air, I blurted out the information I knew and stormed out. Halfway down the hallway, I heard the detective's voice yelling after me. Even though I didn't want to, I halted. Every piece of me wanted to continue walking away, getting as far away from him as I could. But that wouldn't have been fair to April. When I turned around, to my surprise, the detective stood in front of me appearing chagrin.

Apparently, my precise description of the lake spawned enough interest to listen. Once his mind opened to the possibility that I may know something, he began the search. Three hours later, they found April's body. After all the hype settled, the detective never once apologized for his rudeness toward me. Instead of being angry, I found enough justification in knowing I helped lead them to April's killer.

The pressure from wondering how well I'd be accepted by Nicole's uncle was strangulating. When things were out of my control, I usually didn't let them consume me, but this meeting had to go right. Detective Tanner disbelieving me wasn't an option because Johnny's depending on me. I couldn't disappoint him.

The heaviness filled my chest as the anxiety kept rising. This was the time I usually grabbed my cigarettes, and I yearned for that stick that was buried deep inside my handbag. I could practically taste the menthol as I blew away the built-up anxiety. *Yes, I could definitely use that cigarette.*

Either from the lack of sleep, or the fact that I disliked police stations, the walls started closing in on me. The pressure in my chest tightened, forcing me to concentrate on my breathing. If I didn't get out of this room soon, I'd go insane.

To keep my hands from fidgeting, I played with the handles on my bag–twisting them around like a never closing twist tie. It didn't occur to me that squeezing my handles to death could be viewed as another form of fidgeting. When I added the tapping of my foot to my constant twisting, Barry had enough. He reached over, placing his hand on top of mine. My hands stilled from the slight pressure applied. I jerked my head, having every intention of protesting, but stopped short.

He regarded me with such tenderness that I was mesmerized. As I stared in the depths of his eyes, the warmth that spread through me hinted that everything would be all right. His demeanor brought out a smile, and I glanced downward as my cheeks started to glow. The kiss we shared last night crept into my mind, causing my cheeks to burn. I tried hiding, but there was no concealing my reaction towards him.

Out of the corner of my eye, I noticed Nicole eyeballing back and forth between Barry and me. Clearly witnessing our exchange, she smiled coyly, while giving me wink. This caused me to blush deeper, if that was even possible. The distractions worked, because I wasn't destroying my handles anymore.

The receptionist's dull voice sounded heavenly when she announced the detective was ready for us. After jumping up rather quickly, I practically sprinted toward the doorway. Nicole and Barry scurried to catch up to me, but I realized I had no idea where to go. Reluctantly, I slowed my pace to let Nicole lead us to her uncle's office.

"Nicole, it's good to see you. Please take a seat," her uncle said with a warm smile as we filed into his office. "Now, what can I do for you and your friends?" he asked as we sat down in the chairs lined in front of his desk. An extra chair must have been brought in, placed in between the permanent ones, because it clearly didn't match. Plus the extra seat made it crowded in here.

"Hi, Uncle Steve, we want to talk to you about the Johnny Matthews case."

Her uncle, raising his eyebrows, seemed clearly intrigued. "What about it?" he asked with a certain level of dryness to his voice. Cleary shifting away from the friendlier tone he spoke in just seconds ago, I could tell he suddenly became serious.

"We've discovered something that may…help." Nicole answered, glancing nervously back at me.

"Detective Tanner, I'm Heather Reiner. I moved here about two months ago into the house on 1214 Maplewood Drive." I interjected.

"The Matthews old residence, yes…I know it well. I'm failing to see the connection, though. Did you find something relevant to the case?"

"Sort of…Are you familiar with the term clairvoyance?"

"Sure, people can supposedly see things that happened." Leaning forward in his chair, his eyes narrowed while asking, "What are you trying to tell me, you're a psychic?"

"I'm clairvoyant, seeing things that have happened; I certainly can't predict the future." I corrected. People have such misunderstandings when it comes to the supernatural. He was going to be a harder sell than Nicole realized. "Detective, I worked with the police department back home on case file 3010, April Hartley. If you call detective Perry Jenkins he can vouch for me."

Trying to sound as professional as I could, I added, "I believe I know where Johnny's buried."

"How on earth could you know that? We searched and covered this entire town, but didn't unveil any significant clues. He may even still be alive."

It was apparent, he didn't believe his own words, but obviously everyone involved in this case was still clinging to hope.

"My mother found a toy truck belonging to him while cleaning one day. When I reached to pick it up, I had a vision of him being abducted, and then later killed."

Shutting my eyes for a second to recollect my thoughts, I slowly reopened them. "In the woods, behind my house, he is buried in a small clearing."

"You know where this is?"

"Yes."

"You saw him buried there?" he asked as he stared straight at me.

Hesitating slightly, I managed a weak yes.

With the detective still staring intently at me, I swallowed as sweat beads started forming on my forehead. My pulse quickened while the intensity of his glare increased. He was intimidating as he sat there analyzing me. I was sure he noticed my falter since I didn't actually see Johnny get buried, but I certainly couldn't tell him I retrieved his location from a ghost-like figure.

All credibility would surely be lost.

Not sure whether he believed me or not, I started to feel anxious under the scrutiny of his stare. Finally he leaned back in his chair and pulled out a recorder.

"All right, start at the beginning, and tell me everything you know."

After explaining my visions in detail and telling him where they could find Johnny, he leaned forward in his chair raising his hands up to his face under his chin. I took this as a good sign since he seemed to be mulling over all the facts.

"You didn't see the killer's face?" he asked after a long pause.

"Not exactly...I know it was somebody he recognized, but not anybody who was close to him. For some reason I can't see his entire face, but I did get a good look at his eyes." A shiver jolted through my body as I recollected the thought. "His eyes are brown, along with his hair. Detective, I believe I know who did it, a Mr. Barton. I didn't witness him abduct or kill him, though, but I can't shake this feeling that he's involved."

"Mr. Barton? Yes, I remember him. He was very cooperative, and even helped with the search parties. His record was clean when we ran it last. Why do you suspect his involvement?"

"Like I said, it's a feeling." As my eyes dropped, I stared at my hands. I wish I didn't have this strong premonition about him, but something was off. *Why would he have false identification in his possession hidden like that?* I didn't want to present that information yet because last I knew breaking and entering was still frowned upon.

"It's just a feeling I have. I can't really explain it." I stated instead.

"Are you a hundred percent sure where Johnny's remains are?"

"Yes."

"You seem pretty confident in your answer. This task you're asking us to do won't be easy. If you're wrong..."

"I know. But I also know I'm right," I declared, gazing directly into his eyes with all the assurance I could gather. One thing I knew was to show confidence in not only what I claimed, but also my supernatural ability. If I appeared weak, he'd never believe or take me seriously.

Letting out a deep breath, he glanced downward toward his desk. Contemplating what I said, he returned his gaze to me, saying. "Okay. Let me do some checking and I'll contact you tomorrow."

"Thanks sir," I said.

Extending his arm out to shake, I sat there studying his hand. "Sir, I mean no disrespect, but I have to decline a handshake. I'm afraid you've seen too much for it to be a peaceful exchange."

As if understanding, he slowly placed his arm down, but studied me as if I was a microorganism under a microscope before nodding. "Tomorrow then."

As I stood up to leave, I turned back toward him and said, "Detective, another name thrown at me was Christopher Warfelt. I wasn't sure who that was, or what it means, it's just another piece of this bizarre puzzle that doesn't seem to fit anywhere, yet."

He nodded his head as if to dismiss us, and we turned to leave. Nobody said a word until we were out of the police department, walking across the parking lot to Barry's car.

"Do you think he believed us?" Barry asked as we approached his car.

With a sigh I said, "I don't think he believes in the supernatural, but I think he's curious enough to at least follow through with the info we've given him."

"Heather, you were very convincing and professional. You definitely captured my uncle's interest—that's not easy."

"I hope you're right, Nicole." As I slid into the front seat, I added, "We have nothing to do now but wait until tomorrow." Silence dominated the drive home as we contemplated what tomorrow would bring.

14 Discoveries

"**O**h come on, meet us at *The Gamer* tonight," Caleb pleaded.

Friday had arrived and school was letting out. Barry was going to chauffeur Nicole and me home. As the three of us were piling into Barry's car, Caleb stopped us. His ultimate goal for the evening was talking Barry into going out with the guys.

Being a local hot spot, *The Gamer* was known for its popularity among local teens. The draw of the pool tables and various types of games lured them in. Its reputation preceded itself because enough people have talked positively about it. Popular or not, I would never voluntarily visit. I'd spent my whole life avoiding these types of places and didn't plan on changing any time soon. By the uninterested expression Barry held, I didn't think he wanted to go either—at least not tonight anyway.

"Not tonight but soon, though," Barry said, casually confirming my suspicion.

Before he gave an answer, I knew he'd turn him down. Caleb was unaware of the plan the three of us had previously made. Our plan, exclusive to us, meant Caleb wasn't going to get his wish. Earlier, we decided to hangout with each other tonight, thinking we should be together when the detective called. If he called with anyone else around, questions would surely be asked.

We'd been on edge throughout the entire day. Since we were unable to converse at school, our nerves were shot. At least mine was anyway. Worry began settling in my stomach around lunch when I began wondering if the detective would follow through with the information. Figuring we would've received a call by now, I'd become more worried with each passing minute. The quicker we leave this school, the better I'd feel. I assumed Barry and Nicole were anxious to talk too.

Last night Barry decided he would spend the entire weekend at his grandma's house to be accessible. Nicole had the same thought because she was coming over to my house to spend the night. When we were devising our plan last evening, she came up with the suggestion. I was eager to have her stay. Excited even. Shamefully, it would be the first time anyone spent the night. When I was younger, the girls would talk about their slumber parties they'd attend. When I knew of one going on, I would lie in my bed, wondering what it would be like.

My mom's face was priceless when I asked her if Nicole could stay over. Her eyes bulged out from shock before regaining her composure, quickly agreeing. It was hard keeping a straight face watching her reactions. Truthfully I didn't need to ask, knowing full well she wouldn't care, but part of me wanted to see how she'd react. She didn't disappoint.

"Seriously, dude, tonight's going to be tight. You need to be there," Caleb said a little more cajolingly, but I think he knew the battle was being lost.

None of their friends knew what was really going on. We hadn't discussed keeping it a secret from them, but Barry certainly knew where I stood on the subject. The fewer people who knew, the better. Nicole held true to her promise of not telling anyone as well. Thoroughly impressed by her loyalty, I felt like she more than deserved my trust now.

I'd admit, having two people I considered friends was strange. Although nice, the skepticism still hovered in the back of my mind. I wasn't used to having one friend, let alone two. Sometimes I was still paranoid, though, always waiting for something bad to happen. Like in algebra, when you take a positive and multiply it by a negative, the outcome was always negative. Maybe I'd always have trust issues, but at least I was trying, which was a big step for me.

Climbing into the back seat of Barry's car, Nicole rolled her eyes at me as Caleb kept pleading. Suppressing a smile, I slid into the front seat as Barry slapped his friend on the back, saying, "Some other night, I promise."

"Fine...If you change your mind, you'll know where to find us," he finally conceded. He shook his head while walking away, clearly disappointed.

"If you really want to go, I can call you when I receive some information," I teased him as he got inside his car, shutting the door.

"Not a chance." Grinning, he cocked his head toward me saying, "They'll be all right without me tonight."

While holding his gaze for a minute, I smiled back. Something about his smile was just tantalizing. I fantasized about his lips closing the gap between us, brushing ever so softly against mine... My phone rang, breaking me out of my fantasy. Pulling the phone out of my pocket, I glanced nervously at Barry before answering. My voice was a bit shaky, but Detective Tanner didn't seem to notice. He started talking right away, getting straight to the point. As I sat there quietly listening, two sets of eyes penetrated straight through me.

"Yes sir...Okay...No...We'll be right there." I sighed as I hung up the phone.

"Well? Don't make us wait. What did he say?" Barry asked.

"Did they believe us? Are they meeting us there?" Nicole anxiously asked at the same time. Her question made me pause. She asked if they believed *us*, like we were a team. I wasn't sure how to process that because no one ever included me on a team before.

"Yes," I stuttered. "He asked me again if I'm one hundred percent sure where Johnny's buried. He said he called the detective back home and was impressed with my help on the case. They thought it would be best if they go ahead and proceed. There's a unit that's going to meet us at my house and then I'm supposed to lead them to where he's buried."

Resting my head against the headrest, I closed my eyes. This was actually going to happen. Soon, it would be over with. The thought of knowing there was a chance my nightmares might end was such a relief.

While my eyes were still shut, the gentle pressure from Barry's hand as he placed it upon my knee sent a shiver along my left side. I opened my eyes, turning toward him, giving him a grateful smile. He didn't offer to remove his hand, and I must admit it felt nice having it there. It made me feel secure.

Again he seemed to know exactly what I was thinking as he said, "It's going to be over soon."

I remained quiet as I sat there continuing to stare at him. He always puts me at ease by knowing exactly what to say or maybe it was his touch comforting me. Either way, I was thankful for it.

Nicole was in the back seat talking animatedly, but I wasn't really paying much attention. My mind was consumed with thoughts of Barry. After this case is resolved, I kind of wondered if we'd be able to find some type of common ground to keep us together. Johnny, in a sense, brought us close together and after he leaves, I hoped our bond remained strong.

Turning onto our street, I was amazed by the amount of police cars lining the sides of the road. With the lights flashing brightly and uniformed policeman standing around, it resembled a scene from a movie. We glanced at each other, but remained quiet as we crept slowly along, pulling into his grandma's driveway. Looking toward his grandma's house, I noticed her peeking out the front door, her face scrunched with concern. My heart broke at seeing her worried expression. I believed it aged her by at least ten years.

"Barry, do you know what's going on?" she questioned as he got out of his car.

He ran over to her, and I heard him start explaining as Detective Tanner made his way over toward me. Her audible gasp shot pains through my heart. This poor woman had to relive the awful moments of Johnny's disappearance again.

"Okay, Heather, this is your show now. We'll have you lead us to where you think he's buried. After we get there, then I'll have my team start digging until we find something. Are you ready?" Detective Tanner asked candidly.

I nodded, not saying a word. With a glance toward Barry, I noticed his grandma staring over toward us with her hand covering her mouth in disbelief over what he told her. As he leaned to kiss her cheek, I heard him say "it will be all right" before jogging over toward us.

Much to Detective's Tanner dismay, I lagged for a couple of seconds to give Barry time to catch up. I certainly didn't need Barry with me, holding my hand, but excluding him wouldn't be fair. He deserved to be a part of this, as much as I did, especially since he'd been with me from the beginning. For him to miss any part of it now would be a crime.

As I rounded the corner of my house, I picked up my pace as Barry had caught up to us. Noticing the driveway was empty, I breathed a sigh of relief. Mother must have been working late tonight, which actually worked in our favor. It would have been a shock to her having everyone here without knowing what was actually going on. I hadn't told her anything since the night I asked for the truck, nor had she asked. Since she had no intentions on discussing it any further, I never felt the need to disclose anything.

As I led everyone to the clearing, Barry was beside me, with Nicole not far behind. We walked together in silence, too deep in thought to carry on any conversation. I kept thinking about the huge burden I shouldered. My nerves made my stomach clench in knots, but I couldn't think about that now. I had to keep pressing forward for Johnny.

All of them needed some type of closure in their own way, but the one person I didn't want to disappoint the most was Johnny himself. He'd been silent for ten years, and his chance for his voice being heard was now.

I couldn't help but feel a little eager that his time had finally come.

Stopping short as I reached the edge of the clearing, I glanced toward the detective, asking him to give me a moment. Nodding in agreement, he waved his hands, motioning everyone to back up a little and informed them to keep quiet. Barry motioned to Nicole, and they backed up, too.

Taking a deep breath, I stood there for a second, closing my eyes to clear my mind. I knew the location already, it wasn't something I could easily forget, but I needed to be precise. Who knew how many times they would try if by some chance I happened to be wrong. With my arms extended slightly, I slowly walked over to where I knew he lay.

The feeling I had the last time kept getting stronger the closer I got. It was like an energy field that started in my legs, rising upward through my body, cutting off my airflow. When I practically stood over him, my chest tightened to the point I could hardly breathe. Getting down on my knees, I touched the ground. Immediately, images of Johnny were flashing in my mind.

"He's here. He's right here," I gasped out, when I was able to speak.

With each struggling breath, the pain in my chest seemed to grow stronger. My body started shaking, either out of pain or fear. Black dots started impaling my vision. I was going to pass out. Arms gently wrapped around me, trying to help me up. Realizing they belonged to Barry, I leaned my head against his chest as I tried to breathe. He kept whispering reassurances, but I couldn't quit shaking. The image of Johnny's killer coming at him kept playing in my mind.

The complete terror I knew Johnny felt was finally too much for me to bear as the tears I'd suppressed began falling freely. Barry squeezed tighter, no doubt trying to make me feel better, but I knew those images would haunt me for the rest of my life. No matter what they found.

As Detective Tanner and his team came over to start their procedures, the detective asked, "Are you going to be okay?" Replying with a nod, Barry and I backed out of their way and went to stand with Nicole. As we approached, her face wore the same streaks as mine.

Without giving any thought, I reached over and grabbed a hold of her hand. All I wanted to do was comfort her. Luckily I didn't incur any visions, but I couldn't believe how careless I'd become around my friends. Friends…a word I never cared for was now the best word in the dictionary.

Thinking again how much things had changed since I'd moved here, I was in awe. Never before did I ever willingly touch anyone. Now with a friend in need of comfort, the fact that I automatically reached over and grabbed her hand was almost unbelievable.

The longer we stood there watching them set up, the more tired I became. Maybe because I was at the point of being totally exhausted or slightly overwhelmed, I didn't know, but I needed to sit down. Running on just a few hours of sleep for two consecutive nights was taking its toll, and I could feel myself withering away.

Catching Barry's attention, I tilted my head toward the log that I'd grown accustomed to. With a slight nod, we walked over there in complete silence. This silence wasn't one of deep thought, though, this was fear. Fear that any sound we made would distract them while they worked, disrupting the whole process. As quietly as possible, we inched our way over there.

Once we were settled on the log, Nicole reached over and squeezed my hand, whispering "Thanks." I just smiled back. Now, knowing how much this means to her, I was glad Barry had decided to tell her when he did.

All three of us sat there completely stunned at the scene unfolding before us. They took their time, I presumed, to not disturb any kind of evidence. It was strange seeing everyone work in synchronization, though. Everyone had a specific role, and it was orchestrated well. As astounding as it was, I wished they could work a little faster.

It was grueling sitting there, doing absolutely nothing, knowing that a little boy had been buried there. This need to go over and help kept brewing inside me, but I had to remind myself my role was done. I was to lead them there, which I did. Now, there wasn't anything else for me to contribute, but to be patient and wait.

Although it seemed like a long time had passed, it really didn't take too long before they unearthed the first bone. The moment that happened, all digging came to a halt as they called Detective Tanner over to examine. After reviewing what they discovered, he glanced over at me before turning back, saying a few words to the team.

As they went back to work, we continued sitting there still afraid to speak. I felt like we discovered the main part of the puzzle, revealing the completed picture. When they unearthed more of his body, Detective Tanner came walking over toward us with a scowl upon his face.

"Heather, I need to talk to you," he said sharply.

Barry eyed me questionably as I shrugged in response. Not knowing what he possibly wanted, I got up and walked over toward him.

"How did you know he was buried here?" he asked rather sternly.

"I told you, through my visions."

"Are you telling me he was still breathing when he was buried? That he was buried alive?"

Cringing at his words I stated, "No."

At that point I knew he'd figured out it couldn't have come from my vision since Johnny was already dead when his killer brought him here.

"How did you know?" he asked more harshly.

Barry stood up, and I shot him a warning glance before responding. "It was a feeling...a...a very strong feeling. I led you to believe it was through my vision so you'd take it seriously. I'm sorry I misled you, but I just knew he was here."

"Like the feeling you have about Mr. Barton?"

I swallowed hard. "Yes."

"Shit. Come with me," he demanded as he started walking out of the woods.

With a glance back at Barry and Nicole, I pleaded silently for them to follow me before taking off after the detective. When I heard the rustling of the leaves underfoot, it gave me great comfort as I continued walking after the detective.

I wasn't sure what Detective Tanner's next move was, but I guessed it had something to do with Mr. Barton. I much would prefer Barry to be with me in any kind of dealings with that awful man.

Arriving at the detective's car, I stood by in silence, waiting for Barry and Nicole to catch up with me. Barry came over and wrapped his arms around me as we waited for the detective to finish running Mr. Barton's name again on his computer. Frustrated that nothing was showing up, he glared over at Mr. Barton's house. His eyes shifted into a squint as he seemed to be studying it.

His voice rang out loud as he stated, "You kids wait here…I'll be right back." He got out of his car rather hastily and took off in the direction of Mr. Barton's house.

As we glanced at each other nervously, Nicole's panicked voice interrupted our exchange. "Why is he going over there? Does he think he's involved?"

"He probably wants to question him, or maybe feel him out, but I don't think he's home. It appears pretty abandoned." Barry said as he grabbed a hold of my hand.

I knew he was thinking the same thing: Mr. Barton had probably already left town.

We stood there quietly until the detective came back. Wearing the same scowl on his face, he mumbled something about this not feeling right and got back on his computer.

"Heather…What was the name you gave me the other day?" he growled.

"Christopher Warfelt?"

Without any kind of response, he immediately started typing in the name. It took a minute before information started flowing in. Creeping toward the door to get a closer peek, I held my breath afraid to look since I wasn't sure what to expect. As the screen flashed in front of me, I was shocked as the information become visible.

Christopher Warfelt was a seven-year-old boy reported missing about fourteen years ago. His case was classified as open since it had never been resolved. Glancing over to Barry, our eyes locked together as an unspoken understanding passed between us. I briefly wondered what I'd gotten involved in since this became more complex by the minute. As I stood there trying to process everything coming across the screen, all the color drained from my face as a photo of his suspected murderer flashed onto the monitor. It was the longest second of my life as we stared at the picture. Once the initial shock wore off, all hell broke loose.

The name of the photo was Joseph Banks, but there wasn't any denying it. The image in front of us was Mr. Barton, but with bleached hair. As Detective Tanner scrolled to the next photo, the close-up sent a shiver right through me down to my core, for those eyes were unmistakable. Even though I felt like I knew all along, this picture finally confirmed it.

As soon as our brain processed this information, Detective Tanner was on his radio calling it in, and the search was on to find Mr. Barton.

"Dispatch we need to put an APD out on a Daniel Barton. Suspect 5'11", mid-sixties, short gray hair, brown eyes with glasses. Possible... Driving a Chevy Astro Van Blue in color..."

As his words were fading in and out, Nicole broke down and started crying. Her composure was completely destroyed by this point, and I thought to myself that she wasn't made for this type of life. She should be happy, living the normal highs and lows of high school drama, not this. I had to give her credit, though, because up until now, she'd been holding up pretty well. Barry gave my hand a squeeze before letting go and went over to console her.

As we kept standing there, my emotions started to wear on me as well. Part of me felt empathy for Nicole, but the other part felt relieved since we were close to finding Johnny's murderer, but something else nagged at me. Then it finally occurred to me. We knew he had another form of identification in his house the other day, but didn't know why. I thought, what if...

"Detective..." He jerked his head toward me as I began to explain how we broke into his house and found the second identity he had.

When I got done explaining, he simply told me, "We'll discuss the breaking and entering later." Then he immediately went to his radio, putting out the word of his possible second alias.

Wondering if knowing his alias will help track him down more easily this time, my thoughts were interrupted by the smooth, female voice ringing through the scanner. "All units we have a 207 for a Ryan Boyer. Amber alert has been issued for a Ryan Boyer, seven years old, last seen walking home from school wearing…"

My heart sank as I processed the new information blaring across the radio. I knew Mr. Barton, or whatever his real name was, would be behind this. It fit his pattern. He preyed on seven-year-old boys, the sick bastard. Knowing this literally made me sick to my stomach.

My head started to spin, but I couldn't move, unbeknown to my surroundings. I felt as if I was miles away, alone.

"Heather…"

I heard my name being called, but I couldn't respond. All I could think about was a little boy who was out there with that horrible creature. God only knew what the poor boy could be thinking or going through right now.

Flashes of Johnny's face as he caught sight of the knife played through my mind. I felt like screaming…That poor kid.

"Heather…I need your help."

Snapping out of my thoughts, I turned toward the voice calling my name. "Yes," I finally managed to speak.

"Heather, I need you to go with me over to Ryan's house. I think you might be able to help. Do you feel up to it?"

"Sssure," I stuttered as I walked around to the side of his squad car. With a glance back toward Barry and Nicole before taking off, I gave them a weak smile. They

stood there staring wide-eyed at me, slowly raising their
hand   to   wave   good-bye.

15 Questioning

As we pulled up to the Boyers' driveway, I wished my friends were with me. It was a strange feeling, since I'd always been independent, but it would have been nice to have Barry hold my hand while I went inside their house. Or at least have his company. I wasn't looking forward to the anguished faces of Ryan's parents and didn't want to face it alone.

Detective Tanner was still with me, of course, but he wasn't helping my nerves any. He kept telling me what to focus on as if I didn't already know.

I wasn't sure how my life became this complicated all of a sudden. I'd never had it easy, but this was rather intense. I longed for normalcy.

My mom was very mistaken, thinking our move would be a simple fix for my problems. When she arrives home tonight from work, she was in for one big surprise. I knew Barry would be there to explain, but since I hadn't told her much about Johnny, she wasn't going to be very understanding. I hoped she wouldn't worry about me, especially since I wasn't at home where she thought I was.

As the front door opened, my breath hitched as remorse extinguished anything joyful. We were greeted by a very solemn-faced, stern looking man I assumed was Ryan's father. The expression upon his face was exactly what I dreaded. If Barry was there holding my hand, I'd probably squeeze too hard, but it would have let me channel some of this heartbreak.

After Mr. Boyer opened the door to let us in, I could tell instantly these were very religious people. On the wall, as we came into the house, a huge iron-rod cross greeted us, along with a framed picture of Jesus hanging adjacent to it. Other than that, the walls were pretty bare, except for a painting of the last supper hanging on the distant wall.

Sitting on the far end of the couch with a bible in her hand was Mrs. Boyer. She resembled the typical Sunday school teacher, long skirt, hair fixed in a bun, appearing like she couldn't hurt a fly. She didn't have the normal glow they usually have; it was replaced with pain. It was heart-wrenching to see her anguished expression.

I figured she wasn't getting much support from her husband since I pegged Mr. Boyer for a typical "I'm the man; therefore, I'm the boss" type husband. The one support she seemed to be getting was from the bible she clutched in her hand.

Detective Tanner got straight to the point right after we stepped through the door. He immediately started talking to Mr. Boyer and jotting down additional information. Sometimes, I thought, he came across as callous, but I guessed it came with the job. Nobody would want a softie detective working their case, but there should be some type of balance.

The detective began explaining my involvement when Mr. Boyer's eyes snapped up and glared at him. Then with a quick jerk, his eyes scowled at me, for a couple of seconds before landing back on the detective. His expression shifted from a somber one to anger. I couldn't understand what the detective said to cause this sudden change.

The moment after mentioning the possibility of envisioning where Ryan could be, he leaped forward and immediately starting yelling, "Get that witch out of here. I don't want any kind of black magic performed in this house."

"Mr. Boyer, I assure you Heather is no witch. She doesn't perform anything ritualistic. She has a special gift that allows her to see things beyond the norm. She is the reason we have our single lead," Detective Tanner quickly said, coming to my defense.

I stood there numb from shock. Of all the hushed whispers and backlash I received back home, not once had I ever been called a witch. The thought never even crossed my mind, and I wondered how he drew that conclusion. Afraid to move, I watched Mr. Boyer pace back and forth as he continued his rant.

"I don't care what you call her. Anyone who possesses those types of powers isn't welcomed here. That's the devil's work and we won't have any part of it."

"Mr. Boyer…"

"No," he yelled as he turned and glared at me. His eyes, boring into mine, were venomous. "Get out of here," he continued to demand.

I stared at him in disbelief and then turned to leave. I didn't get far before his wife spoke up.

"Richard," she screamed. "Let her try…If it has any chance of helping…I'd sell my soul to the devil himself; I swear…" Her voice broke as she began to sob.

"Judith, I don't…"

"Richard," she pleaded, interrupting his rant. "Let her try."

Mr. Boyer's face morphed into complete shock mixed with rage. Guessing Mrs. Boyer didn't speak out too often, I wasn't surprised he seemed completely appalled by her outburst. What surprised me was his rejection of my help.

If it had been my son missing, I'd go to any length to find him.

He opened his mouth as if to speak, but quickly closed it before storming out of the room. Mrs. Boyer broke out into sobs, clutching the bible tight to her chest.

Not quite sure what I should do, I thought maybe it would be best if I just did what he wanted and leave. As I inched my way toward the door, Detective Tanner motioned for me to stop, whispering to wait a minute. I froze in place, afraid to move again, wishing for some small miracle to get me out of this never-ending nightmare.

Physically and emotionally drained, all I wanted was to go home and sleep. My bed sounded so good to me right now. With one glance at Mrs. Boyer, guilt sprung forward making me ashamed of my thoughts. I had the luxury of going home, but her little boy didn't. Acknowledging that put it into perspective, reminding me as to why I was here. With a new determination, I was going to help whether they wanted me to or not.

Immediately, I started searching for something that could have belonged to Ryan, something he would have treasured. There just wasn't anything lying around for me to find, their house was extremely tidy. The hallway probably led to his bedroom, which I thought would be a good place to start. Not sure where my boldness came from, but nobody, not even Mr. Boyer, was going to stop me from helping that boy. Taking a couple of steps toward the hallway, I glanced once again toward Mrs. Boyer when I spotted a ragged, tan leg.

Coming to a halt, I paused before moving closer in hopes of a better view. My suspicions were confirmed– the leg belonged to a stuffed, bunny rabbit. Elation sprung up for I knew that had to be one of his favorite toys. The material was far to worn for it not to be. The velveteen had lost its sheen and was matted in areas where the stains had been too much. Staring at it, I knew it was exactly what I was searching for.

"Mrs. Boyer...Is that bunny one of Ryan's toys?" I asked as gently as I could.

Tear streaked eyes swept toward me while slowly picking the toy up. "Yes, it's his favorite," she whispered. With a pained expression, she glanced back down at the toy. A sob erupted before she added, "They found it lying next to his book bag on the...sidewalk." She could barely speak, she was shaking so badly.

It was excruciating, listening to her anguish, knowing she had every right to be worried. If Ryan was with Mr. Barton my mind couldn't even fathom what he was going through. Other than incurring the vision, I had no idea how to console her.

My head turned as the detective came over and kneeled beside her. While staring at her, he spoke softly. "Mrs. Boyer, we will try everything we can to bring your boy back safely. Okay?"

She closed her eyes, barely nodding.

"One thing we want to attempt is to have Heather try to see where Ryan is. She has a real talent for this sort of thing. Do you think she could hold the rabbit?" he asked.

With a slight hesitation, she lifted her head toward me asking, "Would you like to see it?"

While making sure there was plenty of space between us, I sat down beside her, slowly extending my hand. "Please, if I may."

As she handed me Ryan's toy, I closed my eyes. My fingers felt the rough edges of the matted velveteen as I squeezed my fingers around it. The image of a blond, curly haired boy came into focus…

Walking along the sidewalk, with his book bag on his back, he glanced hesitantly at a blue van parked along the street. It was the same van he saw yesterday parked in that exact spot. He thought it was strange seeing it again because it's never been parked in this area before.

With a quick dismissal of the thought, he began to slow his pace as a wave of fear passed through him. He was walking by a two story house with a black wrought-iron fence in front of it. He stalled for a minute as he stared at the house. His gaze lingered on the high peaks and angled windows as if they scared him. The house was intimidating, and looked like it belonged in a scary movie set.

My body jerked as it became difficult to breathe. Cuddled in the backseat of the van, he labored for his breath as fear overpowered him. Tears streamed down his face while confusion swirled around his brain, wondering what was happening. His mouth hurt from the duct tape over it, but he couldn't pull it off because he was tied up with a rope.

As he lay there frightened, he sought solace from the flashing lights passing by. They were pretty. It occurred to me they were taillights from across the way. He turned back toward the front of the car, but quickly looked away. The sun sat low in the sky, blinding him. While continuing to watch the red flashes, the lights of the city faded behind him… As I snapped back to reality, I figured out he was on a busy road like an interstate.

When I reopened my eyes, I quickly said, "He was kidnapped in front of a two story house with a wrought-iron fence in front of it. There was a blue van parked along the curb." I glanced at the detective and said, "Like the one Mr. Barton drives." Pausing for a second, I continued, "He wasn't concerned about the van because he was too scared of the house. He's still alive, but they're heading away from here. They're on a split road like an interstate."

Mrs. Boyer let out a gasp as Detective Tanner came over and asked in his serious tone, "Do you have any further details about the surroundings?"

I squeezed my eyes shut, trying to remember anything important before adding, "The city lights were fading. I can't see much from the backseat, but I'm on the driver's side, watching them grow dim. The sun is too bright when he looks forward, so he keeps staring behind him. There are taillights from the other lanes of traffic that I could also see."

"Okay...They're probably heading west," he mumbled as he darted out to his car.

Standing up, I peered over at Mrs. Boyer, who was staring at me with widened eyes. "You could see him? He's...He's alive?" she managed to choke out.

As I peered into her eyes, my own started to glisten. The last thing I wanted to do was give her false hope, so I stated my next sentence carefully. "It's not an exact science, but yes, I did see him alive."

I left out the fact that he was bound and gagged, which made me feel guilty, but she didn't need to know that part. No mother wanted to hear that, especially about their own child.

Somehow managing a weak smile, she thanked me as I got up to leave. I hoped we would find him still alive because nobody deserved to suffer that type of anguish.

Knowing that Johnny was kept alive for a while before Barton killed him gave me hope, but I wasn't sure if this time would be the same. I hoped they'd be able to stop him before he could do any more harm to Ryan.

As I walked out the door, I thought about Mr. Boyer again. It seemed strange that he never reappeared; however, I was glad because he would have been in the way. Maybe if he was reunited with his son, he'd view what I could do differently. Part of me didn't believe that, but I was glad to at least help Mrs. Boyer and most importantly, Ryan.

I worried about her, though, because if it ended badly, I wasn't sure what type of support she'd receive from her husband.

As I got into the car, Detective Tanner was already calling in the possible location of Ryan's whereabouts while I waited patiently as I could for him to finish. Wanting so badly to find that creep, I hoped they'd be able to stop him and quick.

It was hard just sitting there waiting for the detective to finish. Feeling Ryan's fear and confusion outraged me. We had to find him.

"Okay, they have the state police on the interstate covering the exits," he said as soon as he was done. "We're going to get him." Pausing before shifting the car into drive, he stared at me for a moment before saying, "Don't let Mr. Boyer get to you. People say hateful things when they're under distress. I'm sure he doesn't mean it."

With a shrug, I replied, "Thanks, I'm kind of used to being treated like a social outcast."

"Well, it doesn't make it right. Besides, how can it be the work of the devil, when you're clearly helping to put evil people away?"

With a slight nod, I smiled tentatively, wondering if he was right. He remained quiet as we sped away toward some country roads I assumed would eventually intersect with the interstate.

As the scenery flashed before me, I wondered how many people in this town were going to treat me differently after tonight. My guess was everyone, with the exception of Barry and Nicole.

My abilities would definitely be known since hiding them were no longer an option, but it didn't matter. What mattered most was finding Ryan, but the fact tomorrow was Saturday instead of a school day didn't hurt. At least this way, everyone would have a couple of days to absorb the shock.

"We have the suspect spotted at mile marker 140 heading west on I-70. All units proceed with caution, suspect considered armed and dangerous." The screech of the radio rang through, breaking my train of thought.

My heart began to race when the detective immediately flipped on the overhead lights and sirens. The wailing of the sirens alone was enough to get my adrenaline pumping, but watching the flashing red and blue colors dance around us in a circle as he sped to unimaginable speeds was exhilarating. The countryside flashed by so quickly, the scenery became a blur. The thrilling mix of excitement and fear pulsated through me as I grabbed the armrest, hanging on for dear life. For the first time in my life, I was grateful to be wearing a seatbelt.

As we raced through the country roads, I let out a sigh of relief when the interstate came into view. Slowing down to merge onto the on ramp, the dispatcher announced they had the suspect in sight and started closing in on him. It was hard to breathe, fearing for Ryan's safety. I wasn't sure how far away we were, but I knew it wouldn't be too much longer until Mr. Barton was brought down.

16 Negotiations

As we zipped along the interstate, I noticed the mile marker 135 sticking alongside the road. Breathing a sigh, I knew we weren't too far away. The dispatcher had come across the radio announcing they had the suspect stopped between 129 and 130. I wasn't sure how many minutes that calculated too since I was unaware of the speed we were traveling. Due to the other vehicles on the interstate, the detective did have to decrease his pace. At least a little.

I had to admit, I felt a little superior sitting in the squad car, watching people pull over as we passed them. Never having been in this situation before, it was a little intoxicating. I could see why some police officers developed a God complex when they were in that position—it was rather empowering.

With less than two miles to go, we shifted onto the shoulder since the traffic was stopped along the interstate. Each vehicle we passed marked the closeness of our arrival while the anticipation of what I was about to witness spiked my adrenaline.

When we approached the scene, lights from the emergency response vehicles flashed all around. The amount of responders was intimidating. There had to be at least twenty or more vehicles, which more than doubled the amount on my street earlier. Everyone from state troopers and county sheriffs to ambulances and fire trucks were there. By the time we arrived, they had surrounded Mr. Barton's van which was slanted along the embankment.

Pulling up behind one of the parked squad cars, the detective ordered me to stay in the car. As he quickly stepped out, my breath caught, staring wide-eyed at the sight of him drawing his gun. With a clear picture of the pistol in his hand, the reality of the situation brought it into prospective. I knew this was a serious situation, obviously, but seeing it unfold right in front of me was surreal.

At this point, I wasn't sure what was going on. The radio buzzed with different codes, but I didn't understand what they meant. All I could gather was they had him pulled over, and he wasn't cooperating. He seemed to be holding Ryan hostage, which I found odd because he had to know it wouldn't end in his favor. *How could it?* He was completely surrounded by the police.

Even though the situation was far from over, I couldn't help but think the irony of the circumstances. For a little boy to have to go through this was a horrible thing, but also bitter sweet. If he hadn't taken Ryan, then no one would have been searching for him and he may have gotten away. The police certainly wouldn't have beefed up their search for him, and if it wasn't for Ryan's toy, I wouldn't have been able to see where he was. Barton could have settled in the next state, terrorizing another child.

Laying my head against the headrest, I closed my eyes while thoughts of Barry infiltrated my mind. It seemed so long ago since we were all together. Much has happened since, and I wondered what he and Nicole were doing.

Nicole was supposed to spend the night with me, but I bet she was with him at his grandmother's house. So much for my first sleepover. They were probably wondering about us, too. I needed to call them with an update soon.

Upon reopening my eyes, I strained to see if there was any useful information to pass along. The troopers were positioned with their guns pointed toward Mr. Barton's van while a suited guy was apparently trying to negotiate with him. Rolling my window down to try to hear the words exchanged were pointless since I was back too far. I couldn't understand anything they were saying, but I could tell the negotiations were ongoing.

Giving up on the idea, I pulled out my phone to call Barry. Glancing down to dial, I noticed a missed text from him. I guess with all the excitement going on, I failed to hear the message alert. It simply stated, "Call us with an update soon. Be careful." Smiling to myself, I dialed his number.

"Heather, thank goodness. We've been worried. What's going on?" he asked, a little frenzied.

As I proceeded to fill him in on the limited details, I slid back down into my seat, silently wishing this nightmare to end. After explaining everything I knew, he proceeded to tell me they were still exhuming Johnny's body.

He also informed me that Mom had come home, but he was able to explain everything to her. No surprise, it came as a shock to see the emergency vehicles surrounding our house, but he explained the situation before she panicked. Nicole refused to leave until she knew I was safe and, as I suspected, was with Barry. My body relaxed, listening to his smooth voice. It was mesmerizing. As he continued explaining, my eyes closed, allowing his voice to calm me down. Just as my breathing evened out, a loud popping sound erupted through the air. I jolted straight up, dropping the phone into my lap. My relaxed state a forgotten diversion.

Fumbling around trying to pick it up, I could hear Barry shouting, "Heather...Heather...What was that? Are you okay?"

As I peered out the window, everyone was running toward the van. "Gunshot," I finally managed to squeak out. It was terrifying watching everyone cluster together and not know if Ryan was injured. I wanted to get out of the car and go over there, but I would just be in the way. But sitting here was torture as I listened to the officers yell. I shifted to get a better angle, but still couldn't see anything. Then I heard something, and I swear it was the faint sound of my name. Finally it occurred to me that Barry was still on the line. My hand must have drifted down while I was trying to find out what was happening.

Quickly putting the phone back up to my ear, I uttered, "Barry, I'm sorry. I don't know what's going on. There was a shot fired, but I'm not sure who fired it. I can't hear exactly what's happening, and I don't know about Ryan."

"Okay...Do you want me to stay on line with you?"

"No...I'll let you go, but I'll call as soon as I can."

"Heather...Be safe."

"Thanks, Barry"

After hanging up the phone, the confines of the car seemed to be closing in on me. I struggled to sit there as it became more restrictive. Unable to take it any longer, I swung the door open and jumped out. With the crisp evening air, I began to breathe better, but I stayed beside the car.

The wailing of ambulance sirens pierced the night air, making it impossible to hear anything they were shouting. All I could think about was Ryan. He's seven; he shouldn't be going through this. When the ambulance drove closer toward the scene, I stood on the tips of my toes and stretched, straining to see. They pulled out a stretcher and a few minutes later, I breathed a sigh of relief when I saw a male figure lying on it. It wasn't too long after, the detective came walking around the corner with Ryan beside him. He may be emotionally scarred, but otherwise he appeared unharmed.

As I blew out my breath, relief swarmed through me. It was exhilarating to see him safe. I can't see into the future, so I didn't know how this would end. Having it end positively was a great feeling and knowing I was part of the reason was even greater.

After the detective brought Ryan to the car, he introduced me to him, explaining that I was the main reason for finding him. My heart melted as he peered up at me with those big brown eyes, swollen from crying. He smiled partially, but didn't utter a sound. All I wanted to do was reach out and give him a hug, but I didn't dare. Touching him would certainly lead to having a vision, especially with all the turmoil he went through. To keep from frightening him more, I maintained a safe distance.

"Okay, Ryan," Detective Tanner said as he placed him in the back of the car. "Let's get you home to your parents."

A timid smile spread across his face as he nodded, but his eyes held an underlying terror to them. Curling up in a ball, he wrapped his arms around his legs. Witnessing him sitting there took all the strength I had not to console him in some way. It was heartbreaking seeing him still pain stricken. His face streaked from all the crying and the red marks surrounding his mouth from the remnants of the tape made me sick to my stomach. I wanted so badly to offer some sort of comfort, but didn't know how to go about it.

I realized the more I let people in, the more complicated life became. I wondered, as the detective drove toward Ryan's house, if my life would ever go back to the quiet seclusion of before. I didn't think that was possible.

17 Reunited

If I thought I felt elated at the sight of seeing Ryan alive, it was nothing compared to the sight of him reuniting with his parents. As we pulled up to the Boyers' driveway, his mother came running out of the house with her arms spread apart. Ryan's face lit up the moment he caught sight of his mother. Watching his face transform into a huge grin with saucer-sized eyes was priceless. It was something I would never forget.

As soon as we stopped the car and Detective Tanner let him out, he sprang from the back seat, running straight into his mother's arms. Mrs. Boyer was crying, but these were tears of happiness instead of the agony from earlier. Her face was beautiful; it glowed with relief and pure bliss. Mr. Boyer had come outside embracing his son as well, but he still wore that stern expression.

As I stood back taking in the scene, I wondered if that man ever softened.

The detective said a few words to them before we headed to the car. Mrs. Boyer, refusing to let her son out of her grip, thanked me again while her husband stood there stoically. He still refused to acknowledge my presence. Guessing his attitude toward me hadn't changed any, I just shook my head as I turned and slipped inside. I could care less what he thought of me. My vision brought this little boy home safely to his mother, and that I would cherish the rest of my life.

In the safety of Detective Tanner's car, exhaustion overcame me. I couldn't wait to get back home and finally sleep. Although I knew Barry and Nicole would be there filled with questions, I still couldn't wait to get there.

"You did well today," Detective Tanner said as he backed the car up. "That little boy is alive today because of you. I really think the force could use someone with your capabilities, and I'm going to recommend they hire you for cases that could use your help. Would you be interested?"

"Um…" Taking me by surprise, I wasn't sure how to answer. After a few seconds, I finally responded, "I'm not sure. I guess just let me know what they say, and I'll definitely think it over."

"Please do…I have to admit, at first I didn't believe in your abilities. When you came into my office that day, I thought there's no way anyone's capable of that. But you definitely have a talent. Nobody should ever doubt your abilities after this. Johnny's case has plagued me for over a decade, and part of me desperately wanted to believe you. My rational side kept me from fully believing, though. I'm just glad I checked out your background and had enough hope to proceed." Staring straight at me, he seemed to soften a little as he said, "Thanks again for helping me today."

The sincerity in his voice was very touching. Finally managing to tell him thanks, I closed my eyes for a second. I had every intention to call Barry, but the next thing I knew we were pulling into my driveway.

I was a little dazed and confused before realizing I had dozed off. Blinking my eyes, I scanned my surroundings noticing a few squad cars still remained. In the distance was a faint light hovering above the trees in the woods. All of my euphoria seemed to vanish as the realization of Johnny's death came crushing back down upon me. One boy's life was spared, but how many before him weren't?

It didn't take any time for Barry, Nicole, and my mother to come outside and greet us. My mother immediately wrapped her arms around me, and I could see the same relief in her own face as Mrs. Boyer's. I guess mothers would always worry, no matter what happened or how old their child was.

Detective Tanner told everyone about Mr. Barton being shot, that he was wounded, but expected to recover. He'd more than likely be charged with Johnny's death, but they needed to collect some evidence first.

After he mentioned needing proof, the room Johnny was held in popped in my head. "Detective, he held Johnny in a tiny room inside the basement for a while before he killed him. We didn't have a chance to go down there, but I know that's where he was held and eventually killed. I saw that in the vision." Mom gasped as she squeezed me tighter. I had so much explaining to do.

"Thanks, Heather. We'll search the entire house. Don't worry, we'll find something to convict him."

With that he left, walking toward the woods.

Completely exhausted by this point, I let out a sigh. I knew everyone wanted answers, but I just wanted to go to bed. Barely able to stand, I stumbled my way up to my porch, plopping down on the top step.

Nicole decided to go home, knowing how exhausted I was. Before leaving, she came over to give me a hug and thank me. She mentioned that she'd never be able to repay me for everything I'd done.

Deeply touched by her sentiment, I hugged her back, and told her being my friend was payment enough. As she left, she hollered back to me, "Get some rest." Barry had also waltzed over. He leaned in to hug me good-bye, whispering in my ear that we'd talk tomorrow.

Once inside, I let out a deep breath before saying good-night to my mom. I went straight to my bedroom and flopped on top of my bed. Not caring about changing my clothes, I snuggled with my blanket, a little too excited about the prospect of sleep.

I was one hundred percent sure I would have a solid night's rest since everything was resolved now. *What more could Johnny possibly want with me?* Closing my eyes, I drifted quickly off to sleep.

So much for my assumption, I thought, as Johnny stood before me.

This time, the dream was completely different. He stood in front of me with a white glow surrounding him, peering at me with his icy blues. As our eyes connected, he smiled really wide. "Thanks" echoed through the air before he evaporated into the light.

Immediately waking up, I scanned my room. There wasn't anything there except total darkness. But I wasn't anxious. Instead, there was a peacefulness that pulsated through me. It was as if his soul had finally been released, and he wanted to thank me before going up to the heavens, or wherever you go after you die. One thing, for sure, this experience has taught me there definitely was an afterlife.

Lying back down, I closed my eyes with a feeling of serenity, drifting off into the best night's rest I've had since moving here.

Grateful that today was Saturday, I woke up around noon. As I sat up in bed, I took in my surroundings. My room hadn't changed since Mom repainted, but for some reason, it seemed brighter this morning. It was as if a huge weight had been lifted, and I grinned at the thought of finally having my room to myself.

Though I was content to stay in bed the rest of the day, I reluctantly got up.

I found Mom in the kitchen fixing her lunch as I poured myself some milk for my breakfast. I knew she must be dying to ask me tons of questions, so I sat down beside her.

Strangely, she remained quiet until I finally spoke.

"What all happened while I was gone?" I asked out of curiosity.

"Well, I came home and didn't know what to think when I saw all the cop cars. Of course, my first thought was something must have happened to you." She shuddered at the thought, but continued, "Barry and Nicole were waiting on his grandmother's front porch and immediately came over to explain what was going on. Although knowing what happened helped, it was still hard for me to calm down, knowing you were out there with some crazy lunatic."

Watching me, she softened her tone before asking, "You've been having nightmares about the boy? Johnny?"

With a sigh, I answered, "Yes." Then, I proceeded to tell her about my dreams. I could tell by her facial expressions she was uncomfortable hearing this, which was why I hid it from her in the first place. I had to give her credit, though, because she actually sat there and listened. I guessed maybe we were making progress after all.

My former therapist would be proud.

When I was through, she simply said, "Ah baby, I'm sorry this happened to you. I had no idea it was that bad. God, I feel awful since I'm the reason we moved here in the first place."

"No…Mom, this was the best decision you've ever made," I interrupted, surprising myself with the declaration. "I mean, look at what we've accomplished. We solved a ten-year-old homicide, reconnected a missing child with his parents, possibly saving his life, and I've made actual friends. Real friends. I would have still been isolated back there."

Tears welled up in her eyes, but these were tears of pride. She reached over to give me a hug and simply said, "I love you."

"I love you too, Mom."

It felt strange saying those words to her because I hardly ever said them. I knew my mom loved me, but she didn't express it much. Part of it was my fault, because I didn't let people get close to me, but I'd never felt unloved. Maybe misunderstood, but never unloved.

I had to admit, it felt good hearing it.

"Oh, before I forget…Detective Tanner called me earlier and wanted me tell you there was a reward for information leading to Johnny's whereabouts. He said the reward was for fifteen thousand dollars, and Johnny's family wants you to have it."

Stunned, I gaped at her in disbelief. After a couple of seconds to recoup, I repeated, "Fifteen thousand dollars?"

She nodded saying, "That's what he said."

"Wow." I didn't know what else to say. "Mom, I don't feel right taking that money. I shouldn't be rewarded that much. I didn't do anything."

"Don't sell yourself short. If you feel that uncomfortable about it, I trust you'll be able to think of something to do with the money. Think it over, honey."

"Mom, Detective Tanner has asked me to do some consultant work if the need arises. How do you feel about that?" I asked, anxious to hear her opinion.

While I sat there quietly for a second, I wondered if she was going to answer. Finally she spoke, "Well I'm not sure I like you being a modern-day Nancy Drew, but I suppose it would depend on the case."

"Who?" I asked.

"Nancy…Oh, never mind," she grunted. With a slight shake of her head, she came over and kissed me on top of my head before heading out toward the backdoor. Still shocked from the news about the money, I rose up a little dazed and went to get ready for the day.

18 Let Down

As I took my shower, I stood there longer than usual, soaking up the warm water as it beat into my back. The tension I'd been carrying for the past month soothed away as the water dripped off. I imagined all the negativity and worry being washed away, swirling into the dark abyss of the drain. When I exited the shower, I was completely refreshed from the inside out.

Drying off, the reward money laid heavily in the back of my mind. As tempting as it was to keep it all to myself, I wondered if I should share it with Barry, and Nicole. It was, after all, a team effort.

Part of me wanted to keep the money intact in order to do something useful with it, like some type of memorial in Johnny's honor. There had to be some good use for it, something that everyone could benefit from.

Surely they wouldn't be opposed to that. No, I think they would love that idea. I just needed to come up with something that would be spectacular.

After wrapping the surrounding towel, I wiped the steam off the mirror and stood there. With my reflection beaming back at me, I studied myself. My appearance was never a concern for me. I'd always fixed my hair to be presentable, but it never went beyond that. Now, as I stared, I couldn't help but wonder what people saw as they looked at me. *What does Barry see?* I'd never cared before until now.

Truthfully, I'd never cared since I thought I'd always be alone. Not once did I ever picture myself with friends, let alone the possibility of a boyfriend. At my other school, nobody would give me a second glance, even before the big freak show. Afterwards, I was taboo. Although I hated it, I grew to accept the fact that my life would be one of solitude. The desire to be pretty? Not ever a concern.

Funny, how things changed. As I viewed my reflection, I noticed my hair needed trimmed and styled. I should also let Mom show me how to apply make-up, which would thrill her. I'd never worn it before, and I briefly wondered if Barry liked girls who wore make-up. *What a silly question. Of course he would.* Most girls did wear it. I just wasn't sure how I would look with it.

The faint ringtone of my phone chimed through the air as I started to comb my hair. I tossed the brush down before rushing into my bedroom. Quickly snatching it up, I couldn't help but smile at Barry's name displayed across the screen. *What the heck is wrong with me?* There wasn't any reason to feel this giddy. But for some reason, the simple knowledge that Barry cared about me, stirred my insides.

"Hey, are you finally up?" Barry asked.

"Yes…I was just getting dressed. What's going on?"

"Just waiting for you," he answered jokingly, but something was off with his voice. There seemed to be an underlying tone of sadness to it. "Can I come over and pick you up now?"

"Um…sure," I stammered out. Catching another glimpse of myself in my dresser mirror, I panicked slightly, realizing I looked like a drowned rat. Not the impression I wanted to go with. "Um…Give me about ten minutes. I just got out of the shower."

"Okay." He chuckled.

After hanging up the phone, I rushed around as quickly as I could and got dressed. Racing back into the bathroom, I hastily brushed my hair before placing it into a ponytail. There wasn't any time to be nervous, but for some reason my heart was racing. The anticipation of seeing him made me excited, and I couldn't wait to talk to him. There was much to tell. First, I wanted to fill him in about last night, and second, I couldn't wait to explain my dream.

As I finished, I glanced one more time in the mirror. I was far from presenting my best, but there wasn't any time to care. I'd just have to work on improving my appearance a different day.

I hurried into the kitchen to inform Mom about leaving with Barry. Right as the words left my mouth, the doorbell rang, sending a jolt of excitement through my body.

I tried not to run to the door like an adolescent child. Instead, I walked as fast as my legs would carry me. Once I opened the door, the sight of Barry brought a smile to my face. He had his back toward me, but he was still handsome as ever just standing there.

"Hey," I said as he turned to stare at me.

"Hey." Catching sight of me, a tiny smile spread across his face, but his eyes didn't match the sentiment. They seemed to be weighted down with the same sadness that laced his voice earlier.

It was peculiar seeing him struggle with maintaining a happy persona. Every time I'd been around him, he was always upbeat, greeting me with his boyish, grin that I'd grown to love. With the whole ordeal being over, I expected him to be in a better mood. Clearly that wasn't the case. Brushing the worry aside, I offered to let him come inside, but he made no attempt to move. Somewhat puzzled by his aloofness, I noticed his car running in the driveway.

"Did you want to go somewhere?" I asked and then remembered he did say he'd pick me up. But he was so quiet; I'd ask anything to try getting him to communicate. *What on earth was wrong with him?*

With a shrug, he finally spoke. "I'd thought we could go to the park and talk." Glancing toward Mr. Barton's house, his eyes slanted into an evil glare. "I just need to get out of here."

"Okay, let me grab my phone," I said in a cheerful tone, trying to mask my concern.

As I went over to pick it up, I genuinely felt sorry for Barry. Still coming off my high from bringing Ryan home safely, and knowing that Johnny's finally free, I'd neglected Barry's feelings. I wanted to kick myself for being too insensitive. It had to be difficult for him every time he glanced at that house. Especially after learning that the entire time they searched for Johnny, he was in the house next door.

As I turned back toward him, I smiled tentatively as we walked toward his car.

19 Realizations

With the drive to the park short, our conversation was light. In fact, we hardly said anything at all. The only person talking was me, and all I asked was if the park was very big. With a nod, he replied, "It's decent." Without contributing anything else, worry began to set in.

When we pulled into the parking lot, Barry killed the engine. Sitting there for a second, he sucked in a breath, and let it out slowly. *What the heck is going through his mind?* The way he acted, I couldn't tell what kind of mood he was in. He seemed...depressed. Hopefully, he'd open up to me soon because this silence was beginning to wear on me.

After I let myself out of the car, I walked around to where he was standing, waiting for me. When I rounded the quarter panel, he took off walking without me. I had to quicken my step in order to catch up with him.

This wasn't like Barry. He'd always been considerate to me. Today, he was cold and distant, making me wonder if he wanted to break-up. One problem with that, though, we weren't actually going together. In fact, we still haven't been on an official date.

Maybe with all that happened, it was finally too much for him, and he wanted to disassociate himself from me. That had been a concern of mine from the very beginning. And who could blame him? I certainly couldn't. Hanging around me wasn't fun, there are too many issues. I admit, I wasn't the easiest person to be around.

A lump formed in my throat at the possibility he brought me here to tell me good-bye.

As we continued walking along, my stomach knotted at the growing suspicion. Not only was the silence stifling, but his lack of physical contact also contributed to my worry. His hands were deep seated in his pockets, making no attempt to hold mine. Since my very first encounter with him, he'd always found some excuse to touch me. His absence of touch only heightened my nerves.

My joyful mood from earlier quickly faded away as suspicion and doubt crept in the further we walked beside each other. Tears threatened to surface, but I blinked them away. The last thing I would do was cry in front of him.

When we came across a perforated metal bench nestled under a maple tree, Barry went over and sat down. Before I joined him, I paused, examining his features. Staring straight ahead, his eyes were still a turmoil of thought. Unable to make out those thoughts, anger began to surface at his continued silence. If he wanted to end our friendship, he needed to get it over with.

Humoring him for now, I settled beside him. Refusing to be the first person to talk, I panned the area noticing for the first time how nice this park actually was. It was decent sized, offering plenty open areas for people to play, or whatever. The area we walked passed was the baseball fields, which were kept in decent shape. The playground was off to our left. There was a section dedicated for smaller children, but the equipment was older. Regardless, there were kids running around playing. Straight ahead were pavilions for family gatherings with trees spread across offering shade. This was a beautiful park. One I could've enjoyed more, if I wasn't worrying about Barry.

Suppressing a sigh, I waited patiently for him to speak. My anger dissipated some, but nothing could tone down that rising anxiety. He'd speak when he was ready. I just needed to give him more time. The birds chirped in the background, along with the laughter from children playing. I tried utilizing those sounds to ease my apprehension, but nothing helped. The knot in my stomach kept growing as each second ticked by. Five grueling minutes passed before he finally spoke.

"Heather," he said. "There's so much I want to say, but I don't know where to begin."

"Why don't you start by telling me what's bothering you." Afraid the answer was going to be me, I held my breath, waiting for him to speak.

His mouth slightly turned up. "That obvious, huh?"

"Something's got you down. I just don't know what, exactly," I whispered, trying not to sound pathetic.

As he turned to look at me, his eyes softened. His hand reached over, grabbing a hold of mine. While intertwining our fingers together, there was no denying the sensation flowing between us. I couldn't be the only one feeling this. I bit my lower lip in preparation for what he was going to say next.

The seriousness expressed across his face made my heart break. I wanted so badly to erase his pain. He continued focusing on me as he said, "You will never know how much I appreciate what you did. When Johnny disappeared, my "perfect" world was ripped apart. I learned at a very young age how vulnerable we all are, and I think it changed me." With a drop of his head, he released my hand during the process. As he brought both his hands to his head, he groaned, "Tough lesson to learn, but an effective one."

"Barry, I'm sorry this happened to you."

As he shook his head in disgust, his voice raised saying, "I don't want any sympathy...I'm not the one who suffered."

He quickly closed his eyes, but not before I caught the sparkle of tears starting to well up.

I leaned toward him, placing my hand on his back. Gently rubbing him, I said, "Barry, don't do this. You can't blame yourself for being the one who survived." I'd heard of survivor's guilt before and wondered briefly if he was experiencing it.

Upon opening his eyes, he glanced at me before turning his head. I almost didn't recognize him because his eyes were fiery. His pupils had dilated to fill his eyes with blackness, making me internally cringe. It killed me, seeing him hurt like this. "You know what makes me sick?" he growled. "That creep talked to me, telling me not to worry when he knew exactly where Johnny was the entire time."

His left hand slammed into the bench as he yelled, "God! He was only six hundred feet away, stuck in some pit of a room."

I moved my hand, placing it on his arm without saying a single word. Apparently, he needed to get this off his chest. All I could offer was my support.

After a few minutes of silence, he spoke again. "I really wish they'd killed him when they shot him."

"Yeah...Me too," I stated.

Turning back towards me, his voice cracked when he asked, "So, they have solid evidence against him with Ryan, right?"

"Yes, and I'm confident they'll find something concrete to convict him for Johnny and maybe Christopher as well."

"I sure hope so," he whispered as he leaned closer to me. My pulse automatically quickened at his proximity. My emotions were scattered by this point.

"Me too," I whispered back.

He brought both of his hands up toward my face. As his lips touched mine, my body became inflamed. There was something different about this kiss. It wasn't as gentle and passionate as the others, instead it seemed more demanding. As his lips were crushing onto mine, they moved fervently, wanting more from me. I felt his need through his lips, leaving no doubt in my mind that he still wanted to be with me. His hands slid across my shoulders, down my arms, sending an electrical jolt through my entire body. This desire I felt toward him was overwhelming.

He broke away, panting heavily. While resting his forehead on mine, he whispered, "Thanks."

As I tried to control my own breathing, I mumbled a welcome even though I didn't know exactly what he was thanking me for. It didn't matter at this point, either. I was in the arms of the most wonderful guy I'd ever met and didn't want that feeling to end.

He drew me close to him one last time, squeezing me. Placing a kiss on top of my head, he sighed before asking, "What happened after you left us last night?"

Proceeding to tell every detail that went on, I thought he was going to have another emotional outburst when I told him what Ryan's father had said to me. It was apparent how upset he was, but I kept talking, letting him digest his anger on his own. When I got to the part about bringing Ryan home, it was hard explaining my emotions.

"Barry," I said. "The expression on that little boy's face when he saw his mother was the most endearing thing I've ever witnessed. When they embraced, I swear you could feel the love between them. It was exhilarating."

"That would've been pretty awesome to see," he said. Finally, a smile spread across his beautiful face. After sharing that story, his mood seemed to lift.

"Then, last night, I thought maybe I wouldn't have any more dreams about Johnny, but I was wrong."

His face scrunched together as if questioning my sanity. I was sure he wondered why I'd be excited to have another dream about Johnny. The words began flying out of my mouth so fast, it was hard slowing them down, but I knew once he heard the reasoning he'd feel better.

"Last night's dream was totally different. Johnny appeared in front of me, but he seemed different this time. Like...he was in present form, not from the past. He had a certain glow about him too, which made it seem like he was happy." Pausing for a second, I smiled at the thought before continuing. "He looked at me and smiled. Then he said 'Thanks' before he sort of drifted away." Pausing again to reflect on the memory, the previous excitement I had felt came rushing back. "Barry, I really believe his soul is finally at rest."

Barry smiled and turned away. He took a deep breath in, and let it out slowly before saying, "Thanks, I think I needed to hear that."

I leaned over, giving him a quick hug. After a few minutes, we got up and started walking, holding each other's hand. This was the way it should be, and I felt more confident walking beside him.

As we passed by the playground, I glanced again at their equipment. There were a couple of outdated slides that had been painted metallic silver, but the rust scabs still shone through the bottom. They were nothing spectacular, just a straight shot down, not offering any curves or bends. The swing set seemed all right, but there really wasn't much more to offer the kids. Most parks by now have updated their equipment, but this town seemed to be lagging. Back in my hometown, the city park housed a newer playground complex. It was nice, made from colored steel and plastic. A thought occurred to me—I could use the reward to purchase new playground equipment! The more I thought about it, the better the idea sounded.

"Barry, I forgot to tell you." I turned toward him as I stopped walking and then glanced back at the equipment. "Detective Tanner called my mom this morning and told her Johnny's family had a reward for any information that led to finding their son, and they have offered it to me."

His eyebrows raised in surprise. "How much is it for?" he asked.

"Fifteen thousand."

"Fifteen thousand? Really? Wow, that's a lot of money."

"Yeah, I was thinking about donating it. See that equipment?" I said as I motioned my hands toward it. "It needs to be updated, and it's something that kids will play on for a very long time."

As I turned back at Barry, his face softened. Appreciation flitted across his features as he stared at me intently. I suddenly felt consciousness.

"What?" I asked.

"Nothing, I just think you're about the most selfless person I know. I admire that about you."

I couldn't hide the smile that broke out, as the heat began to rise in my cheeks, forcing me to turn away.

"It's the right thing to do…That's all," I managed to mutter.

With a squeeze of my hand, he said, "That's a very honorable thing to do." With a glance back toward the playground, he added, "Maybe they can have some sort of plaque or something with Johnny's name on it."

"That's a great idea." I didn't tell him I already thought about having a memorial for Johnny. Instead, I decided to let him think he came up with the idea. As I stood next to Barry, I pictured children playing on the new equipment. Goosebumps covered my arms at the thought, and I couldn't wait to be able to get the process moving.

Turning back to me, he drew me in closer to him. "Now Miss Heather Reiner, I do believe I still owe you a date," he teased as he leaned down to give me a quick but gentle kiss.

"Yes, sir...I believe you're right." I said, still smiling up at him. Ready to leave, I started to walk away giving a slight tug to his hand. As we walked to his car, I knew things would be different from this point on. I didn't want to dwell too much on it because I wanted to enjoy the moment for once. And besides, it felt nice walking beside him as the cool breeze hung in the air, hinting that the season would soon be changing.

20 Pep Talk

o, where are you going?" Nicole asked.

"I'm not sure. He wants it to be a...surprise. I do know he's taking me out to eat and then maybe to a movie. I just don't know what restaurant we're going too," I answered as I rummaged through my closet for something to wear. Finally deciding on a light knit shirt that clung to my body, I pulled it from the hanger. While matching it with a pair of black pants, I decided there wasn't anything wrong with wanting to show off my curves. Once dressed, I grabbed the multi-chained necklace that Nicole let me borrow a few days ago. "Nicole, wait a second," I said, placing the phone down. I shimmied into the top and then hooked the necklace in place. With a glance at my ensemble, I mentally nodded in agreement.

Nicole had called while I was in the middle of getting ready for my date with Barry, but I was glad for the interruption. I was beginning to get anxious about our first *real* date, and she was helping to calm my nerves. After this past week, we'd become extremely close. She'd stuck by me through everything, and I was beginning to learn what a true friendship meant. Never having a friend like this before made me somewhat nervous, hoping I wouldn't mess it up.

"I'm kind of excited, though," I continued, replacing the phone back to my ear.

I was, too. After what seemed like an extremely long week at school, I was in for a much needed break. Although, going back to school wasn't as hard as I originally thought it would be. I knew the first day back everyone would treat me differently, that was a given, but what surprised me was the differences in people's reactions. Half expecting everyone to shy away from me—like what happened in Clayton—there were a few, but that was all.

Some people viewed me as some famous celebrity, which in truth made me feel the most uncomfortable. Never one to vie for attention, I certainly wasn't used to receiving this kind of admiration. It was extremely difficult to deal with. But the people, who remembered Johnny the most, were the kindest. I was a little slow to realize I brought closure for them. Once it clicked, then I started to feel better, learning to take it in stride. It was just different, that's all.

Most people were just plain curious. These were the easiest ones to deal with. Once they seemed satisfied with the answers to their questions, they went about their business. This was the group I liked best, for they left me alone.

It was a select few, though, who kept me humble. Those were the ones who made sure I would remember how I was treated back in my hometown. With cold, penetrating stares, they made it known I wasn't welcomed. It was almost comical, but in a sad sort of way. Sort of like a drama in a theater setting which made me think of the two theater masks...one happy...one sad.

Then, there were the ones who wouldn't look directly at me. It was an odd feeling, accidently making eye contact with someone from across the room and watch them jerk their head away as if in fear. Like...if they stared at me for any length of time, they'd turn into stone or something.

I felt like Medusa...

"I don't blame you. You guys deserve to have some fun for a change," she said, snapping me back to the present.

"Boy isn't that the truth." I half-way laughed.

"I know. The understatement of the year considering everything you've been through, but I mean it. Just push everything else aside and enjoy your evening."

"Thanks Nicole. I'll try to do that."

She laughed. "You better. Well, I better let you go so you can finish putting the masterpiece together."

With a chuckle, I replied, "Okay, I'll try. I'll talk with you tomorrow then?"

"You bet. Remember…Have fun!"

After hanging up the phone, I sat there for a minute and thought about the word fun. A humorless laugh escaped my mouth at the thought. *Fun! What does that even mean? Have I ever had fun?* I'd spent my entire life being so disconnected from everyone that I'd never had fun. When I was younger and people came over to play at my house, it still wasn't fun. There wasn't any fun in witnessing a vision about them and then having to worry about them finding out. Heck, even my time spent here had been filled with such turmoil; I certainly wouldn't classify it as *fun.* I wondered if I even knew how to have it. *Was I even capable of having fun?*

I stopped feeling sorry for myself and threw myself into overdrive. While I raced around putting on the finishing touches to my hair and make-up, I kept worrying over things like what we were going to talk about. *Will we have much to say to each other without bringing up Johnny? Will it go okay? Am I going to be boring?* I'm going to boring! I was starting to work myself up again, which I knew was insane, but without having spent too much time alone with him—apart from the whole Johnny experience—I couldn't help but worry.

I paused while I glanced one last time in my mirror and took a deep breath. Hopefully he thought of me as more than just a friend. I was pretty sure he did, especially since he already admitted so, but I wasn't sure if I'd read too much into it. Like it or not, I was starting to fall for him.

21 Confessions

As I sat on the couch anxiously awaiting Barry's arrival, my legs began shaking. That craving for a cigarette sprung forward, reminding me about my hidden addiction. In the past, I leaned on them for support, but some time had passed since my last one. A smile appeared, realizing I no longer needed the security they provided because I had Barry and Nicole's friendship.

I opened my purse and moved my wallet and some papers out of the way until I found my last pack hiding at the bottom. On impulse, I snatched them up and briskly walked toward the kitchen. Placing the pack down on the counter, I stared at it for a minute. The golden color of the carton appeared bright and shiny with the half-torn cellophane wrapper catching the fluorescent lighting. It was tempting, having it sit there. My lack of willpower overcame me as I took one out. While rolling it between my fingers, I placed it underneath my nose. With a deep breath, I inhaled the fresh scent of the tobacco leaves.

The aroma was almost intoxicating, it smelled that good. I relished the moment as the sweet scent lingered in my nose. Closing my eyes, I smiled.

After a few seconds, I let out a sigh and placed it back down with the others. I balled my hand into a fist, and started punching on top of them, repeatedly. I kept smashing them until they were nothing more than a huge pile of tobacco leaves and crinkled paper. Satisfied with my accomplishment, I scooped the mess up and threw it into the trashcan.

There, I thought to myself, that should take care of it. Taking great pride for making a conscious decision to no longer be dependent on those little death sticks, I yelled out a loud—"Yeah!"

The doorbell rang the second after my triumph, which started the heat rising on my cheeks. It wasn't likely he heard me yell, but if he did, I hoped he didn't think that declaration was for him coming up the path. God, if so, I'd be embarrassed. A small chuckle escaped at the thought as I hurried to let him in.

All my apprehension from earlier seemed to vanish the second I opened the door. Barry was standing in front of me with his mouth drawn into a sexy, mischievous grin. My heart fluttered at the sight, and I had to refrain from jumping into his arms. When his warm, hazel eyes connected with mine, the tenderness in them about brought me to my knees. At that moment, I knew we'd be fine.

"Miss Reiner, are you ready to go?" he asked in the most ridiculously debonair voice. I wasn't sure if he was trying to be serious, but he definitely couldn't pull that off.

"Let me grab my jacket," I answered, laughing quietly to myself. I think I was safe. He must not have heard my triumphant declaration.

Once we settled in the car, we talked the entire time. I really didn't know why I was so worried earlier. Every time we'd been together our conversations have been effortless. He was the easiest person for me to talk to. Besides, he'd seen me through my worst times and still wanted to be around me. It was amazing, really.

We started heading out of town, which puzzled me.

"Where are we going?" I questioned.

"We're going to Harrisburg to a restaurant that used to be one of my mom's favorite places."

"Oh, that's nice." Harrisburg was a couple of towns away, about a forty-minute drive. When he discussed taking me out, I didn't factor leaving town. Which was quite silly on my part considering we live close to a major city, the possibilities were endless.

If it used to be one of his mother's favorite places, I wondered why it wasn't now. I really didn't know too much about her, other than that her name was Jillian, and he never mentions her. It occurred to me that I didn't even know what she looked like. I haven't met his mother yet, and she was never over at his grandma's house.

"Barry, when am I going to meet your mom?" I blurted out, more out of curiosity than anything else. I was usually never this forward, but I couldn't stop myself from asking.

"Um…Soon," he said dismissively.

The wavering in his voice was quite odd, making me wonder why he acted like he didn't want me to meet her. *Was he ashamed of me after all?* That certainly didn't correlate with how he treated me alone or at school. He had no problem with me being over at his grandma's house either.

Puzzled, I decided to let it drop. I didn't want it spoiling our first date, and it was pointless to worry anyway. I was sure he had a valid reason, and I'd just have to wait to find out.

The date ended up being one of the best nights of my life. The restaurant he took me to was fantastic. It was a bit on the pricey side, but had this aura of romance to it. The atmosphere captivated me. Never having been on any kind of date before, I wasn't sure what to expect. But I never could have dreamt something this romantic. He probably ruined it for himself because nothing was ever going to top this evening.

The dinner was by candlelight and even though the place was crowded, it seemed like we were the sole occupants. I wasn't sure if it was the positioning of the tables, the soft lighting, or the combination of both, but you couldn't see or hear other conversations around you. It was easy to devote all of my attention to Barry. I thoroughly enjoyed myself.

The waitress came around; it seemed, at the best time. I wasn't sure if she planned it that way or if it was by chance, but either way, it was impeccable timing on her part.

We were sitting across from each other, having just finished our supper. I folded my napkin and placed it gently on the table. As my eyes slowly rose, they interlocked with his. In that moment, a warm sensation ran through me as my pulse rate quickened. I briefly wondered if I'd ever get used to that feeling. His stare was penetrating, yet gentle, making me question what he could be thinking. A little overwhelmed, I had to break eye contact, and look anywhere but at him. With the heat rising in my cheeks, I felt embarrassed by my lack of strength. I smiled as I took a minute to compose myself.

Reaching across the top of the table, he grabbed a hold of my hand. "I love that look," he said with his sexy, mischievous grin back in place. One of the many smiles I'd grown to adore.

I glanced back at him, and smiled more widely, totally embarrassed. But this time, I held my ground. I continued to hold our eye contact while my cheeks were almost in flames.

"Yeah...That look, right there. You're such a strong, independent person, but that expression...It shows your soft, caring side."

"Is that a good thing?" I whispered.

With a tender smile, he answered, "Oh yeah. It's a good thing." While interlacing our fingers together, he continued staring.

I didn't think I'd ever get used to him touching me. The sensation was amazing. That spark that occurred when we touched didn't fade away. Instead, the connection kept getting stronger. I never realized how physical contact between two people felt. At least the contact with Barry, anyway.

"Thanks," I said softly.

"You're welcome." He leaned forward, and I found myself gravitating to him naturally. "Heather, I really like you a lot. I was smitten by you the first day I saw you move in. Then when you sat in front of me in physics class, I thought I was the luckiest guy," he chuckled before continuing. "Of course that quickly ended after you ignored me. I didn't think you liked me. I thought I was hideous or something. Do you remember? I gave you some notes hoping that would be a way of getting to know you better. But when you took them, you didn't give me a second glance."

The blood rushed to my cheeks, which left little doubt about my embarrassment. I smiled wider before saying, "Do I ever. I still feel bad about that, you know. I'm sorry...I just wasn't used to people treating me normally."

With a grin, he added, "Ah, that's all right." He paused for a second as his smile faded into a serious frown. "Heather, I love you. If it's too soon, I apologize. But I know what I feel. I've never felt this way about anyone before, and I believe we have something special. I just wanted you know what I truly felt."

My breath caught as I gazed into the longing of his eyes. His admission threw me off guard for a second since it was unexpected. Part of me wanted to fill the gap between us, allowing us to embrace while he showered me with passionate kisses. That would have capped off this beautiful scene, but I didn't. I wasn't living in a romance novel. Instead, I sat there, replaying the words in my head. My hesitation was making him nervous, and I needed to say something quick. The last thing I wanted him to feel was embarrassment, but the words refused to come. After what seemed like an eternity, my thoughts were coherent enough to speak. While holding his stare, I replied, "Barry, I know my feelings for you run deep. I feel things for you that I've never thought were possible. I cherish the time we spend together, and I hope you realize that." I paused, not knowing what else to add. I stopped short of telling him I love him, but didn't know why. *Do I love him?* I know I cared deeply for him, but love? If what I felt was love, then I knew I wasn't ready to tell him. Not yet, anyway. To express that part of myself scared me, and I couldn't do it. I wouldn't allow myself to surrender to my emotions just yet. He sat there, expectantly waiting for me to continue, but I remained quiet.

"Well…" He straightened in his chair, while clearing his throat. "I was hoping we could take our relationship to the next level. I know it would drive me crazy if I saw you going out with someone else. So…I guess I'm asking you to make it official. Will you be my girlfriend?"

The way he stumbled around on his words were painful for me to watch, but he was cute, sitting there appearing chagrinned. I thought if he knew how I really felt, he wouldn't be this embarrassed. I really should have expressed myself better, but I just couldn't. Hopefully, he'd understand.

"Barry, I would like nothing better than to be your girlfriend. There isn't anybody else I would rather be with." It wasn't an "I love you," but I hoped my acceptance of his proposal would be suffice. The big smile that spread across his face confirmed that he was satisfied with my answer.

The waitress appeared to check on us, timing her arrival perfectly again. Whether it was intentional or not, I appreciated the fact she didn't interrupt us.

We sat and talked for a while longer before getting ready to leave. After we left, we did go to the movies, but I didn't pay much attention to it. Instead, I kept concentrating on the fact that his hand held mine the entire time. I would sneak a sideway glance at him and smile. It felt secure sitting next to him, knowing that he truly liked me for who I was.

Once we got back to my house, he walked me to my door. I wanted more than anything for him to come inside, but it was too late for him to stay. Of course he wouldn't be far, since he was spending the night at his grandmother's house, but it may as well been Siberia for all it mattered. Any place besides mine was too far.

Not ready for our night to end, I reluctantly told him, "Thanks again for tonight. I had a really good time."

"Anytime, Miss Reiner..." He leaned down toward me, softly brushing his lips against mine. As he embraced me, we shared a long, lingering kiss.

Before turning to walk away, he whispered in my ear, "Good-night Heather. Remember I'll always love you."

He gave me a quick kiss on my cheek and left with me staring longingly after him.

22 Reluctance

"What are you doing later on today?" Barry asked as he opened his passenger door for me. School had just gotten out, and he was taking me home, which had been our usual routine since we officially started dating a few weeks back.

As a cold breeze circled through the air, I shivered, wrapping my jacket tighter around me. Although I'd lived in the Midwest my entire life, I'd never gotten used to the cold. "Nothing, just a little homework, I think," I said as I slid into the passenger seat.

Shutting my door, he rushed around the front of his car, jumped inside, and quickly started it. "Let's get some heat going so you don't freeze," he said jokingly. "I thought maybe you'd like to come over to Grandma's for a while. Maybe work on our physics assignment together?"

"I think that can be arranged," I said, smiling back at him. I liked doing our homework together. It made the tedious chore more tolerable and meant I could spend more time with Barry—something I never got tired of.

As we continued the drive home, I peered out the window watching the trees pass by. Their foliage had changed colors, setting the tone for fall. I smiled as the sun shone through the gaps in the trees, making the red and yellow hues crisper. I absolutely loved this time of year. There was comfort to be found in the ever-changing colors. Although it marked the end of a season, and the harshness of winter would deaden everything, the hope lay in the fresh beginnings that spring offered.

That's how I analyzed my life, waiting for the death of my mundane existence to be able to rebirth into a better beginning. I didn't expect it to happen this quickly, but I felt as if I'd been given a new chance at living.

I could just sit back and enjoy what was left of the season since our wonderful fall days would be ending. Even though it seemed like the season had just begun, we were already past its peak. Some of the leaves had fallen already, but soon they would be blanketing the earth, as winter approached.

Pulling myself away from the window, I glanced toward Barry. I was glad he asked me to go over to his grandmother's house because I enjoyed spending time with him. Even if we were just going to be doing homework, we always had a good time when we were together. The one thing that kept nagging at me was the fact that I hadn't met his mother yet. We always ended up going either to his grandmother's house, or mine…Never his own. In fact, I still didn't know where he lived. I tried telling myself it wasn't a big deal, but the question wore heavily on me. Once, when I was alone with Nicole, I came close to asking her if she knew why he would keep me away from his mom, but I stopped myself. It didn't feel right prying into his personal business without his consent.

"You're awful quiet today. What's going on inside that mind of yours?" he asked.

"Barry, do you realize I don't know where you live?" I questioned while watching his face carefully. His smile faltered a little before regaining his composure.

Drawing his lips into his half-grin, he answered, "It's not that exciting."

I waited for him to elaborate while continuing to watch him. When it was apparent he wasn't going to add anymore, I half-way joked, "I still would like to know where you go at night when you leave me."

He drew in a deep breath and released it slowly. "Okay, I'll drive you past it before we head home."

As he turned left, his eyes were weighted with worry as he scanned for traffic. Apparently something's off because he clearly didn't want me knowing where he lived. Although I found that rather strange, I remained quiet. Part of me wanted to tell him to forget it and just head toward his grandma's. That would have been the polite thing to do, but my curiosity was piqued. Polite or not, there was no turning back now.

If I knew *why*, then maybe I wouldn't press the issue. But not knowing where he lived wasn't the entire problem. The fact he didn't want me meeting his mom concerned me. I wondered if he felt I wouldn't be living up to her expectations. Like, I wasn't good enough, or something. Or maybe he didn't think she'd understand my abilities or something to that effect. It could just be that he was afraid of what his mom's reaction would be. Still, I would've felt better if he'd let me meet her, or at least explain to me the reason behind his reluctance to have us meet.

While driving, Barry tried to talk, but I could tell he was apprehensive. I acted like I didn't notice. I went as far as changing the conversation to some silly topic about mating habits of giraffes I saw on the Discovery Channel last night. That resulted in a laugh, but there was still an underlying nervousness to his voice.

Slowing down to a crawl, he pointed over to a one-story house off to my right. Half expecting to see a run-down, weathered home that he'd be embarrassed about, it was instead surprisingly cute. The house was smaller in size, as with most houses on the block, but the vinyl siding seemed fairly new. The yard was nice and neat, properly trimmed. The landscaping was absolutely beautiful with the prettiest flowers I'd ever seen. That house was stunning and eliminated the possibility of him being ashamed. Which only confirmed my suspicion—he didn't want me to meet his mother.

"This is nice, Barry…Thanks. Don't you want to go say hi to your mom?" I pressed, trying to be sly.

"Um…She's probably not home right now," he said rather anxiously. With one last glance toward his house,

VISIONS

he shifted his eyes as he deadpanned, "She usually doesn't get in until late."

It was quite obvious he didn't want to discuss his mother any further. I suppressed a sigh before adding, "Well, thanks for showing me where you live. I think it's cute, and it *is* nice knowing where you take off to when you leave me."

The smile I loved seeing spread across his face as he reached over, grabbed a hold of my hand, and said, "No problem. I don't go far." He gently raised my hand up to his mouth and softly brushed his lips against the top of my hand. "Let's get back home."

Smiling at him, I simply responded, "Okay." I couldn't help but think he references his grandmother's house a lot as *home*. He must prefer being over there as opposed to here. I glimpsed in the side mirror and watched his house shrink in the distance still left wondering why.

As we arrived on our street, my heart skipped a beat when I saw the familiar police car parked in my driveway. Immediately recognizing Detective Tanner's car, I started to worry, wondering what could have happened now. The closer we got, I noticed he was outside sitting on some chairs–a recent addition–talking quite comfortably to my mom. Mom seemed to be listening to him intently, for there was a gleam in her eyes as she stared at him. It was a gleam I'd never seen before. We drove right past, without them giving us a second glance. Some detective, I thought to myself and had to stop the chuckle wanting to escape.

Parking in his grandmother's driveway, Barry got out and walked me over to my house. Although he didn't say anything, I think he was just as curious as I was. As we walked across the lawn, Mom's laugh trickled through the air spiking my curiosity further, for this was out of character for my mother. She was usually quite reserved around people.

When they finally noticed us approaching, the detective stood up rather hastily with a sheepish expression. I wouldn't have ever thought we could have thrown him off guard since he was usually observant, but I think we actually startled them. Perhaps he was human after all.

"Heather…" He cleared his throat. "I wanted to tell you in person that they're going to build the playground equipment with the reward money you generously offered," he said in a rush.

"Oh that's great. Thanks detective, for coming and telling me this in person," I said, instantly relieved it wasn't anything too serious. I glanced over at Mom and noticed her staring rather admirably at the detective. *What the heck?* Thrown off guard, I had to fight to keep my expression neutral.

"That's quite all right; I thought you'd want to know." He snuck another glance over toward my mother and smiled before continuing, "They're in the planning stages right now, and since winter is approaching, it probably won't go in until April. We'll keep you informed of the progress, though. The mayor wants to have a ceremony for the dedication, so I'll have to fill you in with details later."

As I thanked him, I started to imagine what the playground would look like. There were plenty of different styles to choose from, but I could picture one with tunnels and slides. And not just the straight slides they currently had, ones with curves and bends. Just the thinking about it made me excited.

The detective got ready to leave, but before reaching the top step he turned around saying, "Oh, I'll be keeping in touch with you Heather, if something comes in that I need your help on."

"All right," I said, all excitement draining out of me by those few words. I tried my hardest to appear thrilled at the prospect of working for them, but deep down, I didn't want to. It wasn't that I didn't want to help, but it took me awhile to recoup from Johnny's experience. To get my brain back into normal mode, so to speak. Although I wouldn't trade that for anything, it was still exhausting.

"Great, I'll let you know." With one last glance at my mother, he added, "It was nice to meet you again, Ms. Reiner."

"Vicky, please call me Vicky," she quickly replied, appearing rather flushed as a pinkish tone over-took her cheeks.

"Miss Vicky," he said with a nod. And just like that, he was gone.

I gave Barry a knowing look, and he flashed quickly back and forth between Mom and the detective before giving me a quirky, little smile. Evidently, he thought the same as me.

⟨୬୧⟩

Later on that evening, I went over to Barry's grandma's house. I'd been there many times these past few weeks, but I still couldn't get over how sweet his grandma was. She had more or less adopted me, and insisted on me calling her "Grandma," too. When she was around, I did, but it was mainly to appease her. No matter how much I adored that lady; I still couldn't feel comfortable calling her grandma. I never knew my grandparents, but somehow I viewed it as a betrayal. They probably wouldn't mind, even if they were still living, but still.

"Since we need to study, I thought it would be easier if we studied in my bedroom," Barry said, pulling me out of my reverie. He shrugged, adding, "Follow me."

While I tagged along behind him, I realized I'd never seen his room before. We'd always stayed in the living room or kitchen. Instantly, I was intrigued.

Upon entering his room, I was surprised to see it look like a typical teenage boy's room, instead of some stuffy guest room I'd envisioned. The walls had a chair rail wrapping around the room, splitting it in half. The upper part was painted taupe that matched the background color of the bluish plaid wallpaper lining the bottom. The queen size bed sat in the middle along the far wall, covered with a denim duvet cover that matched the blue in the plaid perfectly. Along with a desk, there was a four-drawer dresser with a bookshelf above it. He had sports trophies, along with various pictures and medals, lining the shelves. Upon closer examination, I noticed they were all baseball themed.

"I didn't know you played baseball," I said, wondering why they're kept here instead of at his house.

"Well, when I was younger. Those trophies are mainly from little league. I should probably put them away or something," he said with a shrug.

"No, keep them out. They look good in here, adds character to the room."

I went over toward his bed, placing my book bag down. As I started to get my physics book out, Barry came up from behind, wrapping his arms around me. He lowered his head down to mine, nuzzling his nose in my hair, whispering, "I think you look good in here."

I shivered slightly as goose bumps instantly formed on my skin from the feel of his breath along the nape of my neck. A tingling sensation raced through my body as I yearned to be closer to him. My eyes shifted downward toward his bed, causing my cheeks to flush. They heated a few more degrees as I pictured us taking our relationship to the next level. Knowing full well I wasn't ready for that, nor did I even know if that's what he implied, I remained still while trying to steer my thoughts away. Barry ran his hands down my arms before softly pulling my hair to the side and planting a kiss along my neck. I turned around just as his mouth grazed the side of my face. Our lips found each other as we engaged in a long, lingering kiss. When we broke apart, we were both breathing headily. A coy smile broke across my face as I said, "We need to get busy on our homework before we get too carried away."

Letting out an audible groan, he grudgingly agreed. Once we got absorbed into our work, the electricity sparking between us dialed down a couple of notches. It was enough to allow my mind to concentrate, somewhat, on the problems at hand. But the current continued to linger in the air, making me fully aware of its presence. My mind, a never ending collage of thoughts, kept reverting back to Barry. As I watched him engrossed in his studies, it made me appreciate, again, how lucky I was to have someone like him in my life.

23 Closure

"Heather, are you about ready?" I heard Mom yelling from the front room.

In the middle of applying a pale shade of pink lipstick, I paused, yelling back, "Just a minute." While finishing, I glanced in the mirror, approving my reflection. What a long way I'd come. Never caring in the least about cosmetics before, I had recruited Mom to help. As I stared at my highlighted cheeks and glossy lips, I appreciated Mom even more for teaching me how to apply it properly. Even putting it on lightly, I had to admit, my appearance improved.

I went over to my closet to pick out some flats. A comfy pair of jeans matched with tennis shoes was my normal attire, but I needed to appear half-way decent today. We're going to the dedication for the new playground equipment, which I was sure would draw a large crowd. Barry, Nicole, and I were going to be front and center, and I really wasn't looking forward to that.

No matter what had happened, I still didn't like being the center of attention. It just made me nervous, and I was afraid that would never change. The single attention I liked receiving was Barry's.

While snatching up my shoes, I quickly scanned my room and smiled to myself. I couldn't get over how comfortable I felt in my own room now. When I first moved here, that certainly wasn't the case. The room never quite belonged to me. Not once did I walk in here feeling the sanctuary you were supposed to have when you were in your own space. With Johnny invading my dreams every night, it kept those blissful feelings at bay. But until we solved his murder, I always felt his presence, even if it wasn't on a conscious level.

Now, when I walked in there, that feeling of displacement was gone. Six months has passed since my last dream about Johnny and sadly, I no longer felt his presence. I almost wanted to say I felt empty inside, but that was silly because I knew he was in a much better place. Still…I kind of *missed* him.

I paused at my door, and muttered under my breath, "Today's for you, Johnny." Then I turned and walked out to join my mom.

After arriving at the park, we walked over to the children's playground where the dedication was being held. As predicted, there was already a crowd gathered around, and my stomach did a flip at the sight. I tried to tell myself to calm down, but I wasn't very convincing–even to myself. I didn't understand what was making me so nervous—it wasn't like I had to speak in front of anyone. All I had to do was sit there, along with Barry and Nicole, acknowledging our role in finding Johnny and, of course, donating the money for the memorial.

Still, when I scanned across the crowd, the queasiness wouldn't go away.

Forcing myself to turn, the makeshift stage caught my attention. It was assembled in the front of the new playground equipment. On top, chairs lined both sides with a podium in the center. A smile spread at the view of Barry and Nicole sitting there waving, vying for my attention. In between them an empty seat stood, expecting to be filled by no one other than me. A deep appreciation for them swelled inside at the simple fact of knowing they were waiting on me. Funny how a simple gesture could make someone feel special. With a slight wave in return, I couldn't hold back the smile that spread wider.

On the other side of the podium sat a couple, appearing a little perplexed. I assumed they were Johnny's family. A part of me wanted to go over and say something to them, but I really didn't know what to say. I'd been contemplating the right choice of words the past few weeks, but had come up empty. *What would be the correct thing to say to someone who suffered this type of tragedy?* Fortunately, there wasn't time before the ceremony began, so maybe I'd get inspired afterward. It was a little surreal, seeing this family for the first time, and knowing they gave such a generous gift despite their misfortune. I couldn't imagine how they felt right now.

We finally reached the chairs that were lined up for the audience. As Mom took her seat, I told her good-bye, and hurried over to join Barry and Nicole.

Detective Tanner was standing not too far away; talking to a uniformed officer that I'd never seen before. By their tone, the conversation seemed intense. I didn't pay close enough attention to what they were arguing about since I figured it didn't concern me. Wanting to slip past them unnoticed, I maneuvered myself in a way that drew the least amount of attention.

I talked to the detective off and on during the past six months. There hadn't really been anything significant for me to help with, but I thought he liked to keep in touch in case something did occur. Sometimes, I couldn't help but wonder if his visits had more to do with my mother than me.

When we came home from school one afternoon, they were together on the porch, clearly enjoying each other's company. The reason behind his visit was to inform me about the final details of the ceremony, but the way he was eyeing my mom, I felt he had ulterior motives–After all, everything he mentioned could have been done by phone. As he tried keeping his attention on me, his focus kept straying toward Mom. Shortly afterward, I asked Nicole her thoughts about him, and she informed me he was still married, but they were going through a divorce. Regardless, if he still had a wife, then I didn't want Mom involved. Being caught in the middle of someone else's divorce never ended well.

"I'm glad you're finally here," Nicole said when I reached them. "Can you believe this crowd?"

Her eyes twinkled with excitement, and I couldn't help but smile back—all thoughts about Detective Tanner yearning for my mom erased.

"I know, right?"

Barry grabbed a hold of my hand after I sat down, making me smile. He smiled back at me, causing mine to widen. I just shook my head slightly because he'd never understand how much I appreciated his friendship. He was the first person to break the barrier that surrounded me, and the first person to actually understand me. I admired the fact that he looked beyond my abilities and took them in stride.

Whatever happens between us, I know deep in my heart, he'd always remain a big part of my life. Somebody who had been that open to the strange world I lived in deserved my utmost respect. Although I still couldn't say the words "I love you," he knew my feelings for him were strong. One day, I would have the courage to express myself. Until then, I hoped he'd continue to understand.

With a squeeze of his hand, I turned away to gaze into the crowd. The seats filled up quickly, and I was shocked to see the Boyers sitting in the third row. I couldn't believe they were all here. I never would have thought Mr. Boyer would be anywhere near me. Perhaps he'd warmed up to my ability since his son came home safe that day. His eyes met mine for a couple of seconds, before I had to force myself to turn away. By the fierceness of his stare, it was clear that hadn't been the case at all. *What was that man's problem?*

That cold stare brought back memories of the week after Johnny's body was exhumed. They didn't treat me differently too long, but it was unnerving. After the novelty of finding Johnny's remains and helping with Ryan's safe home coming wore off, most people went back to their normal way of treating me. The difference between the two towns amazed me. Nobody talked to me back home, but here it was so different. I still had the same friends I had before anything became public. Not a single one of them betrayed me.

Maybe that's the difference between a happy ending versus a sad one. Or, maybe it was the simple fact that Barry and Nicole were there backing me up the whole time. Back home, I never really had any friends to stand behind me. It felt nice.

While I scanned the crowd once again, it wasn't hard to figure out that Nicole was right. There were a lot of people here. One person was missing, though–Barry's mom. I had yet to meet her, but I found it strange she would miss this event. *Wouldn't you want to see your son honored?* I had hoped today would be my chance to finally meet her. With Barry spending his weekends over at his grandma's house, the opportunity had never presented itself. I found it odd that she never came around. You would have thought she'd visit his grandma once in a while, but I had yet to see her there. I finally knew what she looked like–sort of. There was a small, oval picture of her sitting on the bookshelf, and I wandered over to it one day to sneak in a peek. The picture was a younger version of her, but at least it gave me an idea of what she looked like.

Whenever I asked Barry about her, it was like driving down a dead-end road. Being reluctant to talk, the conversation fizzled away with me always dropping it. At first I was afraid he was embarrassed for me to meet her, but I no longer think it was me he was embarrassed for. Never wanting to sour our evening together, I didn't press him for information. But before too long, I would have to meet her.

While I glanced toward the right, I noticed the detective was still arguing with that guy. Curiosity finally got the better of me, and I asked Nicole who the person next to her uncle was.

Much to my surprise, her face hardened as she flatly replied, "That's the police chief."

With a disgusted snarl, she turned her head, not adding any more details. The mayor made his way to the podium, so I let it drop. I tried diverting my attention toward him, but out of the corner of my eye, I noticed the detective and police chief parted ways. As Detective Tanner made his way over to us and sat next to Nicole, I didn't miss the scowl on his face. They definitely did not get along.

"Ladies and Gentlemen, I would like to start the ceremony today with a moment of silence for Johnny Matthews," the mayor stated.

As everyone bowed their heads, I kept thinking about the special connection I had with him. These people hadn't talked to him since the day he went missing, but I was fortunate enough to have an exchange with him, just six short months ago. Euphoria tingled through me; the more I thought about how incredible that was. Yes, Johnny, I thought to myself, you deserve this. After everything you went through, you deserved to be remembered.

"Thanks, Ladies and Gentlemen. Today we come together to honor a little boy who was taken away too early from this earth. Ten years ago, this place suffered a horrible tragedy. One of our own went missing. For ten years we didn't have many clues to go on. Six months ago, however, a newcomer came to our town. She brought with her hope…"

As the mayor was giving his speech, I began to feel really uncomfortable. I hated being focused upon. I shifted around in my seat, feeling rather self-conscious as multiple pairs of eyeballs shifted their gaze between the mayor and me. I felt like crawling through the hole in the back of my chair and hiding in one of the tunnels in the new equipment.

Barry must have known how I was feeling because he gave my hand a squeeze. While we sat there, he never let go. He would glance at me once in a while and smile. If anything was going to calm my nerves, it would be him. His warm hazel eyes, with that sexy grin, broke my concentration every time. When he throws that half-grin my way, the background fades becoming my main focus..

People started clapping, interrupting my fantasy about Barry. Evidently the ceremony was over with as the crowd started to disperse. *How'd I miss it?* The mayor backed away from the podium and headed directly over to us.

"Fine job guys…Fine job indeed." He reached out and shook Barry's hand. Then automatically without thinking, he patted me on the back and rested his hand there.

A shiver went through me as the daylight faded away to darkness, revealing me standing in a narrow, darkened street. The area was deserted with tall, but dark buildings surrounding me. On the side of the adjacent building sat a platform, housing a rusty metal door. That wasn't the front side of the building, it couldn't have been. It lacked the welcoming allure that most storefronts had. An alley, I thought to myself, I was in an alleyway, but not alone. The mayor was there talking to some guy who's voice had a familiarity about it, but I couldn't quite recognize. His face, darkened by the shadows, wasn't visible enough. I watched silently as the stranger placed an unmarked envelope into the hands of the mayor. When he leaned forward, enough light filtered through to spark recognition of the police chief. That was why his voice seemed familiar. Uneasiness washed over me as I heard the police chief tell the mayor "This should hold you over for a while."

As the mayor removed his hand, I snapped back to reality. When he started to walk away, I peered at Barry while trying to compose myself. Barry, in a hushed voice, immediately asked if I was all right. With a quick nod, he questioned what I had seen. I opened my mouth to tell him, but had to close it quickly when the Matthews approached us.

"Heather, we could never thank you enough. You'll never be able to know just what you've done for us." Mrs. Matthews said as tears started welling up in her eyes.

"For years there has been a void, and now I think we can start to move on. What you've done with the money was such a noble gesture. His memory will live on forever," she said as her voice cracked toward the end, refusing to let her finish.

While reaching out to give me a quick hug, she whispered "thanks" before hastily walking away. Her husband turned toward me with eyes filled with appreciation, and simply said, "Thank you" before taking off after his wife. Still shaken from my previous encounter, I let out a slight breath. At least her embrace didn't reveal another vision.

With a glance at Barry, I nervously asked, "Did anyone notice me?"

"No, I don't think so. You weren't facing anyone but me. What did you…?"

A flood of people came up to us, interrupting us again. With an apologetic look, I turned back to the crowd and answered the questions being tossed at me from every direction. As I tried my best to listen to what everyone was saying, my mind kept reverting back to what I had seen. I couldn't help but wonder what shady business went down between the mayor and the police chief. Part of me questioned if I should even get involved. I mentally debated whether to tell anyone else except Barry, but something definitely felt wrong.

Standing there having to talk to people was torturous. I tried my hardest to wear my fake social smile, hoping it would suffice. All I really wanted to do, however, was get away from everyone and tell Barry what I had seen. He kept glancing back at me with his own apologetic look, but I knew the suspense was killing him just as it was me. Finally, when the last person left, he came over to me.

"Barry," I said in a low whisper. "You're not going to believe what I saw…"

My mother, who was clearly ready to leave, interrupted us. I groaned before tossing Barry a desperate smile. As he leaned into me, he quickly hugged me while whispering, "I'll come straight over." Walking away, I glanced back toward Barry, knowing once I told him what I'd seen; this town would never be the same.

THANKS FOR READING VISIONS!

Please join my newsletter to get the latest release news at www.kimberlyreadnour.com.

Any questions or comments can be directed to my email: kimberlyreadnour@gmail.com

Please follow me on Facebook at https://www.facebook.com/pages/Kimberly-Readnour-Author/283092008542198

Acknowledgements

Thanks to each one of you, the readers, to have enough interest to read my debut novel. Writing this book has been a fun journey. Originally written for my daughter's eyes only, I am thrilled to have the opportunity for a wider audience. My wish is that you enjoyed the book as much as I enjoyed writing it.

Thanks to my daughter, Logan, for giving me the inspiration to write stories. You helped me discover my passion. With all the hobbies I've tried throughout the years, and there has been many, writing turned out to be the one to stick. I owe that to you. I can never thank you enough to get me to publish this novel. If you hadn't kept pursing after me, it would have continued to sit inside the computer.

Thanks to my beta-readers Staci Vecellio, Brandon Prosser, and Denice Loveless. Each one of you brought something to the story. Staci, you gave me encouragement to follow through with publishing, and to finish the second book. If it wasn't for your encouraging words, I wouldn't have listened to Logan. A big shout out to Brandon for letting me pick your brain for all police material. I'm thankful you're not only an excellent policeman, but also an avid reader. Denice, thanks for giving the manuscript one more read to fill-in any questions. Your advice was invaluable in making the story solid. Thank you everyone!

To the rest of my family, a big thanks for all your encouragement you have given me during this time.

Kathie, my editor, I cannot thank you enough for turning my words into the story it became. A good editor is invaluable, and I feel blessed you were able to be mine.

ABOUT THE AUTHOR

Kimberly lives in the Midwest with her husband and two children. Her oldest is away at college, but when she's home they enjoy hiking, camping, and hanging out as a family.

Made in the USA
Lexington, KY
07 December 2014